ONE
FOOT
IN
THE
GRAVE

ONE FOOT IN THE GRAVE

Peter Dickinson

PANTHEON BOOKS, NEW YORK

LIBRARY OF CONGRESS CATALOGING IN PUBLICATION DATA

Dickinson, Peter, 1927-   One foot in the grave.
I. Title.
PZ4.D55250n   1980   [PR6054.I35]   823'.9'14
79-5354
ISBN 0-394-50894-7

Manufactured in the United States of America
FIRST AMERICAN EDITION

One

HER KISS BURNT on his forehead. Keyed senses, distracted by the powdery odour of shampoo, didn't at once register that the fire was frozen.

"Ice cream for supper?" he murmured.

Her green eyes blinked and widened. She made a face of mock alarm.

"Once a detective, always a detective?" she said.

He replied with a deliberately sleepy mumble, and watched through half-closed eyes as she finished her routine in the room. Everything she did was suffused with surplus life, as though her body was humming with pleasure in its own existence; but these energies didn't spark out of her at random; despite her roundness of feature and general chubbiness, she was no sprawling and chaotic earth-mother, but taut and neat and coiled into herself like the bud of a many-petalled flower—an effect enhanced this evening by the ordered curls of her freshly-washed hair.

He always watched her, for the pleasure of it, but tonight he tried to extract every quantum of life from her presence and use it to feed his own strength. The concentration on her made her seem to be working more briskly than usual, so that it was no time before she stood by the door, slid the light-control down to its night-time dimness, raised her short-fingered hand in blessing, went.

As always her heels clicked twice on the parquet outside the door, and then the thick pile of the corridor carpet muffled her footsteps. He listened for the hiss of the door-push on Mrs Culver's room but it was drowned by a sudden swish of storm against his window. Although he was already clutching the fold of sheet which she had just smoothed over his chest, he hesitated. For so long now in his mind the sigh of the door-push had been his signal to begin that although he knew Mrs Culver's door must have opened and closed it was difficult to move without hearing it do so. All his remaining energies seemed budgeted, so that without the signal he could not find even the tiny bit of moral surplus needed to begin.

The hesitation stretched to a few seconds, then he willed hand and arm to drag the bedclothes aside. He slithered his feet over the edge of the bed and pushed himself slowly up till he was sitting.

So far so good, but to stand he would have to make a single effort—there could be no halfway resting-stage without her arm round his shoulders to steady him. He took two long breaths, clutched the iron bedhead with both hands and heaved, willing grip and arm-muscles to remain taut through the blackness. It came and went with the familiar faint roaring. When it cleared he was still standing, still gripping the bedhead so fiercely that it was hard to persuade his fingers to release their hold. One hand at a time he forced them open and stood unsupported. Excellent.

All now was planned and re-planned, many many times; but the planning had been done in the fragments of coherent thought which were all an old mind seemed able to hold on to at any one time; they were the pieces of a patchwork which he was now stitching into the long-imagined pattern. Each piece as he added it was certain to be slightly different from its planned shape, and so the pattern would grow through cumulative distortions to something, perhaps, he could not have imagined. There was no point in fretting about that now. Too late. Or too soon.

Supporting himself on the bedside table he shuffled round to the wall and picked up the walking-stick from where she always leaned it. Then he crossed to the bath cubicle, opened the door

6

and switched on the light.

When he had first come to Flycatchers he had been barely conscious of what was happening round him, aware only of the change from cold and disorder that had become squalor to a new sphere of warmth and efficiency. His senses had returned to him by fits and starts, until the almost dictatorial precision of the hospital routine had itself begun to seem oppressive. It was then that he had first noticed that the door of the bath cubicle opened in such a manner that it obscured the one-way observation panel in the main door of the room. This welcome flaw in the general gloss and competence had seemed at first simply pleasing; but when he had begun to make his plan, and had realised that he could use the flaw, that had been a good omen. Any of the other staff who glanced in would assume he was using the bathroom. Of course, if she were to come back she would know something was wrong, because she had helped him to the lavatory only five minutes ago; but she wouldn't. She was with Mrs Culver now; then she would do Mr X, and then Lady Treadgold. He knew because he'd asked her, weeks ago, when the plan had been little more than a notion.

"Detecting again?" she had said, laughing with surprise.

"Not at all. I like to know what you're doing, so that I can think about you doing it."

She had laughed again, but told him in detail. He still thought that the second time there had been as much pleasure as surprise in her amusement. As he turned from the doors he drew his pyjama sleeve across his forehead, unconsciously trying to wipe away her good-night kiss, and with it the guilt of deceiving her.

Clothes next. It had always seemed necessary that he should dress himself, though he was aware that his practical reasons were inadequate. Certainly he must stay warm for a while; possibly, if he had the bad luck to be glimpsed by one of the staff downstairs, they would accept that a properly clothed man had a right to be there, but not one in a dressing-gown. But in fact he was determined to dress in order to show that he still could, was still to

7

that extent free.

He shuffled to the wardrobe and slid the door back. By the dim night-lighting he stared at the ranked garments, all strangers. They were of good quality and had been bought to fit him, but he still couldn't think of them as his. Only his hat was a friend. Unplanned, a memory made him pause. *North Kensington, a freezing room, once grand with its high moulded ceiling, now dank, grimy, reeking. Chappie slouched on bed, resigned to arrest. No other furniture, except one chair and one cheap wardrobe, warped beyond closing. Cursory search, nothing there, nothing—paper bag in corner containing sandwich crusts, two empty cider bottles, tangle of wire coathangers on floor of wardrobe and on rail one threadbare black overcoat and one curious dark heavy suit, both doled out from some probation officer's private hoard when the chappie had last come out of nick, five weeks back.* The chappie's face and name and crime were quite lost in the quicksands of memory, but the clothes still floated on the top. He could almost feel at his fingertips the nap of that overcoat and the unwearable felt-like thickness of that suit.

He lifted down one of these overcoats, light but warm, dark blue with a cavalry cut; then a suit of brown tweed. He carried them to the bed and laid them carefully down so that he could slide the trousers off the rail, turn and drop them the right distance from the bed. He fetched socks and a neckscarf from the drawer in the dressing-table, laid the scarf beside the clothes on the bed, unrolled the socks and dropped them next to the trousers. They fell beautifully. Good omen.

He felt his lips twitch in self-mockery. It was five months plus a few days since he'd last tried to dress himself unaided, and by all accounts he hadn't made much of a go of it. That episode too was in the quicksands, but later he had been told that a social worker had found him unconscious, exhausted by his struggles like a fox in a gin-trap, with both his feet jammed fast in one trouser-leg and a long gash in his calf where he'd apparently been trying to cut himself free with his nail-scissors. Ridiculous, and made more so by the attitude of his rescuers, a sense of admiration for the old man, starving, chilled through, delirious, yet still able to try and save himself—just as if he'd been that fox in the gin-trap biting its own foot off to free itself. But they had been right in a way they didn't understand. An element of wildness creeps back into the old, however tamed may have been their workaday lives. He had guessed at it sometimes, a flicker behind the eyes of pensioners as they despaired of explaining their troubles to the desk-sergeant. Now he knew it from the inside. He was wild, and this was a wild night. The last storm of winter.

He nodded, assenting to the omen of the socks and trousers. Pantaloonomancy, that had been his name for it in the days when the way the clothes fell had been an augury for each day's dealings with him. Tonight there would be no debacle, no gin-trap. He leaned his stick on the bed and shuffled round to the back of the chair until he could nudge it on its uncanny smooth castors to the right place by the clothes on the floor, and then returned to its front, felt behind him for its arms and lowered himself. The last six inches went with a rush that made the air grunt from his lungs, but no blackness came. He never normally sat in this chair because he doubted if he could rise from it without help, but his own chair was too high for the trouser-technique. Suddenly he was worried about how this would go; it was something he had barely considered during his planning, because he had done it so often that it seemed to present no problem. Now he saw that five months is quite long enough for a late-acquired skill to rust.

He leaned forward just far enough to see the exact position of the trousers in front of the chair, swung his weight on to his left buttock, used both hands to lift his right leg just above the knee, and swung the dangling foot into its starting place on the trouser bottom. Then the left leg. Fine, but that seldom seemed difficult. Now he leaned his body forward and pulled the waistband of the trousers up his calves until the weight of his feet in the legs stopped him. Next he leaned even further, took hold of the cloth on either side of his right foot and tugged it, one side and then the other, easing it inchmeal under the sole until the foot itself at last crept into the open at the far end of the tube. He rested, gazing at it, as though it were some blind white creature that had crawled out of its cave into the dim light. He was almost unable to feel its existence as part of himself. For all these years it had done its half-share of taking him wherever he fancied, unregarded except when it chanced to send twinges of revolt to the capital brain—corns on those iron miles of pavement in his bobby days, the true pain of a smashed metatarsal when the Islington Rapist had bombarded his besiegers with his collection of erotic statuary. Now it seemed barely governable. Few messages came. But it still lived, as if with a strange, brainless life of its own, a white cave-thing.

He let his foot hypnotise him for less than a minute, then worked its fellow through the trouser-leg. After that came the socks, using the same process. Now came the transition to what he thought of as Stage Two. He sat on the edge of the chair and pulled as much of the trousers as possible right up on to his thighs, so that when he had twisted round to kneel on the floor there would still be enough slack to allow him to fasten the waistband. He straightened, allowed the inevitable blackness to come and go, and eased his buttocks to the chair-rim. Gripping the right arm of the chair with both hands he twisted his legs to the left and started the pivoting movement, forward, round, down . . . Smoothly the chair glided away. For an instant, far too early, he was kneeling as he wanted, but the chair slithered on and he was still clutching the arm until he was stretching like a novice who tries to land from a dinghy and finds himself taut above the water with his hands on the quay and his feet still six feet away in the boat. *Fool*, he thought as he fell. *You forgot the castors.* He heard the thud of his body hitting the carpet and the creak of air compressed through his larynx but felt no pain at all. *Fool*.

He allowed his lungs to gasp and steady before he rolled fully on to his front. He gathered his arms beneath his chest and pushed himself up into a crawling posture, keeping his head hung low to check the flow of blood away from his brain. Crabwise, so as not

10

to drag the trousers back down his legs, he edged towards the bed and hauled himself slowly into the posture of prayer, judging the limit of the blackness all the time and staying outside it. Now he could feel for the waistband, haul it up and with quivering fingers fasten it. Now the zip.

Some mornings those few months back it had taken him almost two hours to get from kneeling to sitting—endless attempts, failures, rests, re-starts. Other days he had achieved it in a single spasm. Tonight two or three failures would be too many.

Still kneeling he sidled to the bedhead, gripped its top with one hand and with the other forced his right leg forward and upward until the sole of that foot was flat on the ground. He rested, gathering his will, and heaved. As the darkness roared through him he used his dying awareness to lean his body forward, and so came to, perhaps only a few seconds later, lying face down across his pillow. Good. Now he twisted carefully on to his back and sat up, judging the retreat of the blackness by habit. After the stupidity with the chair he was back on course. Jacket and overcoat were habit too, tedious but not difficult. His arms were so much better than his legs. He could twist, fumble, manipulate, shrug until each collar nestled against his neck. His hands were scarcely quivering as he tied the neckscarf and tucked it under the lapels to hide the pyjamas. At last he could grip the bedhead as before, will muscles and finger-bones taut, heave, stand.

When the blackness cleared he was in the same position as when he had first risen from the bed, only now he was almost dressed.

He looked at his watch for the first time. Twelve minutes. She would be saying goodnight to Mrs Culver now or perhaps already on her way to Mr X, and she'd spend at least ten minutes with him, prattling away, hoping to extract some new clue to tell her tame detective . . . only I'm wild, he thought. Wild. Biting my foot off.

He crossed the room again and used his walking-stick to hook a pair of shoes out of the cupboard on to the floor. They were the new-fangled sort—slippers, really, without laces—so it was easy enough to prop himself against the cupboard and coax his feet into them. Finally he reached his hat off the shelf and put it on. It nestled round his scalp, familiar, restorative, the only piece of clothing which his rescuers had seen fit to carry over from his previous existence into this one. Its touch seemed to give him not only extra strength and purpose, but even his real identity. He stopped being the vague thing he had been for the last five months—a pity-object, a healing-object, to one person perhaps a love-object—and became a man with a name. James Willoughby Pibble, ex-Detective-Superintendent CID.

Turning from the cupboard he looked at himself in the long mirror. He saw a ghost, the ghost of Jimmy Pibble, the faintest of faint remains of a life once lived. He was standing in the beam of light from the bathroom door, so he was only half a man, all his left side as invisible as the dark side of the moon. The other half wavered in the dimness—face pale as mist, lips a dark scab, no sign of an eye in the deep socket—a creature as weightless as the dry bone of a bird. All that was left. Not long now. The last storm of winter. The cut of the coat added to the ghostliness of the image; if anyone did glimpse him they might well think him a revenant from the days of Edwardian house-parties. The storm whined at a gutter. It was a night for ghosts.

Moving ever more confidently as the plan proceeded without mishap, he took another overcoat and two suits to the bed. He rolled the bedclothes carefully aside and laid the coat and suits down where he had been sleeping. Not enough bulk. Quite definitely walking now and no longer shuffling he went to the bath cubicle and fetched the fat towel and the extravagant sponge, laid them on the clothes and patted the whole pile into shape. He had to brace his thighs against the edge of the bed to pull the bedclothes back over the dummy without dragging it out of shape. All his life he had tended to sleep with his head drawn well down into the bedclothes, and since the plan had taken shape he had exaggerated the habit. She had teased him about it, but he'd simply said the night-lighting disturbed him. And since there was no chance of his re-making the bed to her standards he had coaxed her to stop tucking the bedclothes in. She hadn't liked that. Dangling blankets, all night. Tsk.

"I wouldn't let any of the others sleep like that, you know."

"Why?"

He'd only meant what was the harm in sleeping as one chose, but she'd answered another question.

"Because they aren't really real. So they might as well do things my way."

"Am I real? I hardly feel it, in this place."

"Don't talk nonsense—it's bad for you. Just remember you're real, but the others are all—all gnomes."

"Hobbits?"

"Orcs more likely. Retired orcs. I bet Mr X has got his dragon-hoard somewhere."

How long had all that taken? Another nine minutes. Would she have finished with Mr X? Lady Treadgold refused to be bedded down until two in the morning, and in any case Jenny was frightened of her . . .

Almost but not quite in panic he pushed the visitor's chair into place, shut the wardrobe, crossed to the door and looked round. Anything she wouldn't expect to see? The clothes he'd worn that day were as she'd left them, folded neat as a map on the dressing-table stool. The dummy . . . who could tell? He'd never seen himself from this angle. He nodded to it. You're not real either now, he thought. 'Bye.

He entered the bath cubicle, switched off the light, closed the door to a chink. Very carefully, mistrusting the reliability of touch, he felt his way to the tall stool that stood by the handbasin and eased his buttocks on to it, leaning his back against the tiled wall. A long sigh wandered from his lips. Rubbish, he thought. You aren't exhausted—you've hardly started. Rest. Between three and seven minutes, on previous form.

Now that he was still he became more conscious of the storm noises. Rain turning to snow, the wireless had said. Deep drifts in the north. He had sat in his chair, watching the last light fading, and seen thin flakes like ice-chips beginning to swirl past the darkness of the big cedar. The storm was hissing now through those sombre needles; one of the branches creaked in the gusts. The grip of his will, the impetus of the plan, began to fade and his mind floated into its weary trick of repetition of phrases jumbled beyond meaning or memory of an origin . . . the boiler house is blowing in the wind . . . there's that Frenchman . . . forty-three degrees of thirst . . .

Dark and chill. Waiting, hour after hour, motionless, just in case. Smell of fresh sawn timber and river-reek from the wharf. Unfamiliar constant nudge of pistol holster against ribs. "They might come back," Dickie Foyle had said. "I've a bit of a hunch they won't, but we've got to give it a go. We'll tell the press Monday we've found where it all happened." Two young men had died, very slowly, in this rickety office, their screams drowned by the squeal of the sawmills. No sense of horror or haunting, only the blankness of waiting. No one came. Dickie's hunch right, as usual, but not suspiciously right. Not yet.

The double click of heels on the parquet snapped him out of his doze. He could sense her nearness. She was looking through the panel at the dummy. If it had been him lying there, and if he had still been awake, he would have moved a hand above the bedclothes to acknowledge her watchfulness and then the heels would have clicked and gone; of course, he had no way of knowing how long she waited on nights when he had already dropped off; but tonight she left barely time for the signal to begin before the heels clicked again—a disturbingly unfamiliar sound, heard from this angle—and she was gone.

He felt an absurd rush of disappointment and knew that a large part of his disjointed will had still been hoping that she would notice something wrong with the dummy, would come in, find him dressed and waiting in the dark—and then he would have to explain, and she would understand, and then . . . Deliberately he refused to consider possible thens. Absurd, disgusting. The storm thundered in and out of his mind and left him with regret, now shading into relief and on into vanity that his central will was still in command. No less absurd, but not quite so disgusting.

He looked at his watch and found that his doze had lasted two minutes, so he had barely made it to the bathroom before she had come by. Lucky, again. He eased himself off the stool and leaned his weight on the basin while his legs became used to their function. His shoulders squared. His hand rose unbidden to adjust his neckscarf and hat, just as if he were about to step out and face the world. He left—as easy as that—and without being aware of any conscious decisions, found himself outside his own door, closing it, peeping through the panel at the dummy, grunting with satisfaction, walking down the corridor. The shock of light made him blink a couple of times but did not bother him.

He even took a deep and manly breath, to savour the curiously clashing odours of Flycatchers, the opulence of flowers and expensive perfumes and haute cuisine, all threaded through with the sharp medical smells that arose from the endless, and always losing, battle against old age.

It seemed natural to glance in through the panel of the next door, as if to assert his new apartness from its occupant, Air Commodore Sir Cyrus Turnbull—"My poor old vegetable," Jenny called him. The mimed gesture of farewell stuck halfway through. She was there, standing by the bedside to take the old man's pulse but frowning at the door . . . no, not at it but through it, through him and the wall beyond . . . she had sucked her lower lip under her teeth . . . she looked like a child doing sums . . .

He found he had stopped and was clutching the door-jamb, staring back. It was as though he were truly a ghost now. He could see her, but she could never see him, never . . . and she should not have been there!

He lurched on at a panic shuffle, reached the fire doors and leaned his way through. His stick rattled loudly as it caught in the closing timber. He tugged it free and plunged for the stairs.

Sense seeped back while he stood gripping the banister rail, willing the bubbling dismay to settle. It might be a bit of routine she had forgotten to tell him about. Perhaps she had had to heave the inanimate old hero around while she cleaned him up and re-made his bed, and so could not take his pulse till he had settled—or perhaps she had simply found something wrong on her earlier visit and had come back to check; that would account for her hurrying through with Mr X and Lady Treadgold. Yes, that would be it.

The stairs steadied him still further, a known task. He was strangely fond of them. They were a refuge from the brightness and luxury of Flycatchers, and from the factitious liveliness for which the staff were instructed to strive. There was an aura of deadness and drabness about them which were proper to old age. The same cobweb had dangled from the ceiling for weeks; the carpet was worn; the lower lightbulb had blown and not been replaced . . . As far as he knew he was the only person who used the stairs, originally because the upward rush of the lifts drained his blood from his brain and caused him to black out, but later, as the plan took shape, in training for this one night. He put the training into practice—stick down, left leg down, shift grip on hand-rail, right leg down, stick down . . .

At the fringe of the near dark below the busted light-bulb he stopped and looked at his watch again. Five minutes still before the man was due back—the unseen figure, known only by footsteps, whom Pibble had nicknamed the Liberator. Hamming self-confidence he paced out of the dark, his shoes squeaking on the super-hygienic rubber stuff that covered this lower passage. At the kitchen door he hesitated. Because of the storm-noises he hadn't actually heard the kitchen staff leave, nor the Liberator's first appearance to lock the outer door behind them. All seemed hushed. He opened the door, gave a tiny sigh of relief at seeing the expected darkness beyond, checked his bearings by the light from the passage, and walked in. Once the door was closed he shuffled through blackness until his stick rapped the leg of the big table. Now, as he'd expected, he could see the pale rectangle of the scullery door, outlined by the reflection of the floodlights from the low cloud-layer. Still shuffling in case some stumbling-block lay hidden in the floor-level darkness he moved through the scullery. A jutting cupboard cast a patch of black. During his one reconnaissance visit—affable, dotardly, returning a fork which had somehow got missed from his breakfast tray—he had seen a tall stool standing in this niche. Yes. Perfect.

As he inched his buttocks on to the stool it tilted on some unevenness, only a bit, but enough to make him fling out a steadying arm. His hand rapped against something which itself began to move. Without orders the fingers clutched, caught, closing on a sticky mess. The thing or things stopped their slither and he detached his hand, holding it forward into the faint light, where it glistened with a long smear across the palm. *Blood. Feeling into the waste-bin at the little furrier's. Hand easing down through the cat-like caress of scraps till it touched a different sort of softness. Withdrawing it. Staring at the red smear. Sniffing the known reek.* He sniffed at the mess, touched it with his tongue, smiled at the shock of sweetness and began to lick the mess clean. Raspberry jam and little suety crumbs. Jam roll remains. Staff supper. Yes, he'd almost knocked over a pile of plates stacked ready for Mrs Finsky to come and wash in the morning. That was part of the whole routine, listened for day after day and night after night, studied in the alteration of lights on the tiles of the kitchen courtyard below his window, smelt for, even . . . and now in three or four minutes the Liberator would come across the courtyard and unlock the outer door of the kitchen with a rattle of keys. The mortice, and then the Yale. The door would open, and the kitchen lights go on for a few seconds. There would come the snap of a big switch, the kitchen lights would go out a moment later. Then the man would leave, pulling the door shut behind him, but not locking it. Six minutes later he would return, unlock the Yale, come in and lock up properly. Another switch would snap and the floodlights would go out. Then he would cross the kitchen and squeak out of hearing along the passage . . .

17

Six minutes during which the kitchen door was only locked with the Yale, and so could be opened from the inside without a key.

Rest now. Gather energies. Hardest part still to come. Nearly there, though, nearly there. Deliberately he invited into his mind the retinue of nonsense . . . There's that Frenchman . . . and for many a time I have been half in love with elephants . . . the boiler house is blowing in the wind . . . monosex cricket club . . . there's that Frenchman. The storm boomed. He was half aware of cold, and without thinking about it shrank further into himself, as if withdrawing the frontiers of consciousness to more defensible positions. Like a dance of conjured souls the wraiths of meaning moped and gibbered round and round inside his skull . . . I dare say, I daren't say . . . the boiler house . . .

Cold squeezed in, shaking him from his doze. Had he really slept? The sense of something unfinished was pungent in his mind, like an aftertaste in the mouth. He stood up hurriedly from the stool, bringing the darkness roaring down, but came to and found himself leaning against the cupboard, still mercifully upright. His watch was hard to read in the half-light. He craned back into the shadow, screwed up his eyes and tried to pick out the feeble gleams of luminosity. Five minutes past! The Liberator had come and he hadn't heard! But the floodlighting was still on!

With a lurching stagger he blundered out of the scullery and into the blackness of the kitchen, slowed as though the dark were an actual thickening of the air that clogged his passage, and stood, groping at nothing. A monotonous thin whisper of air squeezed through a crack. He plunged towards it, tripped sickeningly at the door-mat, banged into the door, clutched at nothing but somehow stayed upright. Already, before he had willed his feet into their proper place beneath him, his free hand was patting for the latch. There, now. No door-knob. Higher. There! No grip in fingers, no feeling of shape. Hang stick on crook of elbow, left fingers close on right hand, forcing grip tight, twist with whole body . . .

The storm blasted the door open. Wind thumped round the kitchen like an unleashed dog. He leaned himself round the door

18

and along it, through the gap, tottering against the in-rushing turmoil. A sudden lull almost toppled his forward-leaning weight but his hand was still on the door-knob and he found himself pulling the door shut as if that was what he'd been trying to do. He let it happen. As the catch clicked the storm came howling through the cedar-branches once more.

Clutching his hat down with his left hand he prodded his stick forward, leaned his weight on it, shuffled his feet a few inches and prodded again, God send no gusts from sideways! There were chips of ice in the wind. His eyes raced with tears. The flaps of his coat whipped and wrapped round his thighs, like arms clutching, imploring. He was running into the wind, but making no progress, a race in a nightmare. His heart was talking now, murmuring its little bubble of strain at the top of each pulse, which would be in a few moments a gulp of pain, and then . . .

Then, abruptly, the wind was still. It screamed across the courtyard but he was out of it, standing gasping by a plain brick wall dim lit from an upper window on the other side of the courtyard. All wrong. There was no wall in the plan! And the Liberator! Where was he? In front? Behind? The dream-struggle, disorientation of time and place, seemed to close down completely, but the residual will gave a feeble little shrug of irritation. Somehow it was enough to shrug the world back into place. The fight against the wind had become a fight into the wind, so that instead of aiming at the corner of the garage he had slanted across to meet its main wall. Now he eased his stick into his left hand and with his right elbow propping his weight against the brickwork worked his way along to the water-butt at the corner. Beyond it the floodlights glared. When he huddled round out of the lee of the wall the storm seemed to be made of light. The rain that had fallen all day lay in glittering pools in the weathered hollows of the York paving, but now what was falling was the finest of fine snow, racing in brilliant streaks across the lit arena. Through this dazzling space the colonnade reached out towards the wall of night beyond, and the storm hissed between the square brick pillars as if through the teeth of a vast comb.

When she had first wheeled him round the gardens, before he'd been strong enough to walk more than a yard or two, it had been one of those still, gleaming afternoons peculiar to mid-September. He had not actually looked at Flycatchers from the outside before. The path had turned a corner behind a monstrous hummock of rhododendron and there it was. Amazing.

"Well, that's Flycatchers," she'd said. "Stupid sort of name for it, isn't it?"

"I don't know—old men dozing in deckchairs with their mouths open."

"I'd never thought of that—only the birds. There are lots of them about in summer. They sit on the croquet hoops and make little mounds of doings in the fairway."

"My room's round the other side, I suppose."

"That's right. You have to be absolutely stinking rich to see the Downs from your bedroom. Look—do you see those shutters? They're bullet-proof steel, electrically operated. The shareholders had them put in so that Sheikhs can convalesce here without getting shot at. Why does it always make me think of a ship? It's nothing like, really. Something to do with the tower, d'you think?"

She had been right. A long white building with low-pitched purple slates, large, proportionless windows, a glass-roofed, iron-pillared verandah running half its length, odd niches in the façade dictated apparently by sudden changes of mind about the shape of the rooms within—a typicial Edwardian white elephant, built for the select few to enjoy the douceur de vivre *and now adapted to let their children die pleasantly. There was nothing ship-like about it, and yet it was a great liner, a veteran of imperial cruises, at anchor on this green swell of the Downs. The shared perception made him think of her for the first time as anything other than the neat young woman who made her living in geriatrics.*

"What's the tower?"

"Only a water-tower, but you can see the Channel from the top. It's prettier than the house, isn't it? The ship's gone to Italy, sort of."

20

She was right again. The tower was essential to the image—an Italianate fantasy, a campanile built of different coloured brick in gaudy layers, and joined to the house by a brick colonnade. The sharp foreign accent created the harbour where the ship was moored, Naples, reeking in the sun, displaying its slums to these well-to-do foreigners like a beggar displaying his sores.

Now the ship was moored no longer. The gale made it heave and plunge as he loosed himself from the water-butt and flung himself in a tottering rush for the first pillar. The paving lurched like a deck, but before he totally fell he was hugging the brickwork, hauling himself upright and readying himself, still panting, for the next swirling rush. Miraculously there was a rhythm: it was a game—he was a toy in the hurl and harshness of the wind, but provided he did what the wind wanted it would not hurt him. He used his arms to push off from one pillar across the path of the wind, and let the wind force him back in a staggering curve against the next. The first two were black against the floods, and the third one part of the sudden dark beyond, but even so he seemed to know where it was, to clutch at an exact location in the hurtling blackness and find it still and solid. He felt, but did not see, his hat whirl into the darkness; its going seemed only part of his own. Hat and he were leaves in the wind, weightless, toys of the storm. He was laughing aloud, like a child on a stormy beach, in a high hysterical cackle he had never heard himself make before. When the storm fooled him with a sudden lull, so that he caught his stick between his legs and collapsed on to the paving, he lay for some time, gasping with laughter.

The hysteria died. His body became heavy. The storm was outside him, jostling at flank and shoulders, tramping over his body. His legs were too numb for feeling. Perhaps he'd broken one. Careless. She wouldn't like that. Tsk tsk.

The sense of her disapproval was so strong that he was unaware of forcing his body up on to hands and knees and beginning to crawl along the paving, and then it changed into relief that if he was able to do this he mightn't have broken a leg after all, and she wouldn't be so angry with him. Then he remembered that she was going to be angry with him, whatever happened, and that memory slid him back on to the tracks of the plan. *Nearly there, nearly there*, he mumbled, nodding and grimacing to himself as he inched through the storm.

Something groaned in the wind. Vaguely he'd heard it before, but had thought it was just another storm-noise, a branch of the great cedar near to breaking, perhaps; but now he grasped that it was close ahead, was in fact the door of the tower, wide open, swinging in the wind, hinges groaning. All wrong. Not part of the plan. He shook his head disgustedly, but crawled up the single step and into the tower.

Now he was in unexplored territory. There would be stairs going up—eighty two; the sort of fact people told you. Garden furniture stored. *"It's locked so people don't go jumping off the top, but everybody knows the key's on a nail in the ivy there, so we can get the deck-chairs out. So it's just strangers can't jump. Club members only."*

Out of the wind he was much more aware of the cold. The effort of resisting it had given a sort of illusion of warmth, but now, as he paused to try to guess the position of the stairs, he felt a fresh sense of urgency. His reserves were running very low. Over there, it must be. He crawled across dry paving, brushed against a stack of light wooden objects, followed an apparently clear route, and there, yes, hard and straight as a tree-trunk, the newel of a spiral stair. Twisting himself on to the lowest step he immediately began to climb.

He had invented the technique for himself in his Hackney lodgings. Sit on bottom step; palms on edge of step above; lean back, shove with legs, heave with arms; neat as a tin toy the buttocks slide on to the second step. Hold pose, careful in case the sudden lengthening of the body drains the blood down and brings in the roaring blackness . . . No. Then palms on edge of step above, etcetera, and this time use hands to lift legs on to the first step, so that feet start next cycle two steps below buttocks . . . by

22

the end of his time in lodgings he had needed to rest every three steps; but with returning strength he had worked up to eight at a time in his training sessions on the stairs beyond Turnbull's room. He was not so strong now. Start in sixes. Then . . .

Exercise barely warms the old. Thinned blood moves so slowly through clogged pipes that any heat roused in the central embers is lost before it reaches the remote capillaries. The numbness of his limbs infected his mind. The learnt rhythm, the plan, the will, pushed him up. He shut his eyes to concentrate all his residual forces; as the stair spiralled up a slit of window shone with the glare of floodlighting, but he was aware of it only as the veined and red-blotched smear of his eyelids. He lost count of sixes, rested when the rhythm failed, started again, more urgent than ever. The ghost of reason gibbered that anywhere would do now, but the top of the tower had become his target, set like a footprint in concrete. Reasonless obstinacy, the last right. Exhaustion was itself a good.

The tower had rooms in it. An unimportant detail of the plan had allowed for this, so the first wedge-shaped landing, though it broke the rhythm, didn't surprise him. His mind had forgotten about it, but his body seemed to know what to do, slithering across the flatness and starting automatically on to the next flight. But by the time he reached the next landing he was so deep into the lowest wells of his resources that the alteration was like a break in a dream—the light-glare, the moment of quasi-consciousness, the mumbled query. He stopped. A strange mild warmth swam round him. He opened his eyes and saw through a doorway a bare room lit by the reflected floods. A thin pillared window. A garden chaise-longue—all wrong at this height, like a boat in a tree. On the floor a knot of armoured black, faint-glistening, snake-like. Something else wrong, not in the plan. The smell of the warmth. You feel warm, first time for weeks, when you know you aren't— but that would be a vague glow from inside, surely, not this . . .

The awareness of things outside himself died in a fresh flood of urgency. The top. The top. She had to know he'd got there—then she'd know he'd understood what he was doing. She wouldn't know why, mustn't know why . . . Time collapsed again. The rhythm of work became as involuntary as the double thud of his heart—palms, lean, heave, buttocks, knees. He must have rested, often, but wasn't aware of it, or of anything, until he was roused from the trance by a strange weight on his shoulders, rubbing heavily. A solid upright surface, through which he was trying to climb. Wind shrieking through cracks. Storm-buffet. A door.

There was a door in the plan. Gingerly he twisted into a kneeling posture, rearing his body slowly, cautious of the inner dark. Padlock or bolt? Never been a chance to ask. Pat, pat. No feeling in hands. Sweep arm along surface, up, down . . . there! Lost. Found. Scrabble, fumble. Rage . . .

. . . And he was tumbling, dream slow, into whistling cold. No point in crawling. Just a little further. Slither an inch, clutch at leads, find handhold, pull . . . handhold useless, like slack cable.

Unwilled his hand continued to drag at the loose thing, like a hound worrying some vile object out of a ditch, ignoring its master's shouts to drop it. His eyes opened, as if they too saw no further point in obeying the dissolving centre and had become mere sightseers of this last drama, had found it dull and were looking around for other amusements. They wanted to see what the hand had found.

It was another hand. An arm stretched away from it.

Long idle servo-motors juddered into life, triggered by the signal they had been set to recognise. From somewhere, hoarded against this impossible event, a current of new energy flowed, faint and erratic. He was on hands and knees, crawling forward to see what lay beyond the arm.

The water-tower was topped by a roof like a Lama's hat, supported on barley-sugar pillars. The floodlight, reflected from the white mass of Flycatchers, was caught in the pink plaster vault of this roof and shone dimly down on to the leads. The body lay face up, staring at this pink roof. The handsome mouth sneered at its frivolity. Pibble in turn stared at the body, puzzled, astonished, as the current of discipline faded. He'd done it! He'd brought it off! Pity she couldn't share . . . and how amazing that all that nonsense about an after-life should turn out true! Only . . . Mistake somewhere. Never been a film-star. Never dressed in white lace shirt, breeches, shiny black riding-boots. Typical! Given him the wrong body to hover over. Laid it out neat for him. Might have done something about the back of his head, though. Messy . . . and all wrong anyway, dammit! Didn't they know he had died of hypothermia? All planned. No mess at all. No need for the streak of blood running up across the film-star mask, where they'd turned the body over after bashing the back of its head in. Oh, *rubbish*!

Faintly the current of energy flowed back, aligning chaotic images into a sort of coherence. He wasn't conscious of turning, crawling towards the stair-head, but he could feel his lips muttering.

"The blood's got to get to the brain. That's what matters. The blood's got to get to the brain."

Two

ONLY PATCHES OF numbness. Elsewhere slow aches, unfamiliar sudden pain-bolts, haze, warmth. Hands sometimes, touching near these pain-centres, small hands, round as a dog's paw, assured. Jenny's hands. Her voice too, once or twice, in and out of the haze, muttering, angry, alarmed, mocking. No sense. Dark.

He became fully conscious with unusual suddenness. Without opening his eyes he knew exactly where he was—in his bed at Flycatchers. He felt very sore, and filled with a dull anger that the fulfilment of his plan had turned out to be a long and stupid dream. A fever-dream. He'd been ill. That would account for the aches. Nearly died, perhaps. Typical, you lie snug, dying involuntarily, while in your dream-world you are making furious efforts to kill yourself. Fail in both worlds, too. Typical. Disgusting. He opened his eyes, to distract himself from his inner distress, and saw an unfamiliar presence, a cream and chrome robot glistening beside his bed. Some sort of medical buffoonery. A cable from it was taped to his elbow, and his arm was strapped down. He shut his eyes again. The dream had been very vivid, and unlike most dreams couldn't be teased into fresh shapes by the half-conscious mind. The presence of the robot oppressed him. Either he'd been very ill, or Doctor Follick wanted to impress someone. Or they'd taken her away, and . . .

Next time he woke, it was with more of the usual waverings of reality. She was there, taking his pulse. They'd chopped her hand off at the wrist and attached it to the robot. It was his own hand. No.

"Hello," he whispered.

Her fingers twitched with surprise.

"Oh, Jimmy! How could you!"

"What time is it?"

"What day is it, you mean. You're a stupid old man!"

He opened his eyes. Something was wrong. Over the months a curious grammar had developed, with special moods expressed by tones of the voice, as though their relationship was too subtle to persist in the plain indicative. She was using the indicative now. He took refuge.

"I feel sore," he mumbled.

"No wonder! You can count yourself lucky. If you'd been compos mentis when they brought you in I'd have got out the iodine bottle and done you over with that! That'd have shown you!"

"In?"

"Don't come that. Lying there pretending to be gaga and then . . . Jimmy, did you have to? Couldn't you just have told me?"

"I'm sorry. Thoughtless . . ."

"Thoughtless!" she snapped. "Plain bonkers!"

Her hand was still on his wrist, though she'd lost count, surely. He moved his free hand across to touch it, forcing the movement through a fierce twinge. She frowned down at him.

"What are you going to tell them?" she said. "They're all waiting to see you."

"Who are?"

"Follicle, for a start. He threw a fit. You know that wild look he gets when things go wrong, like a kid at a party getting over-excited. I've never seen him quite so far gone. I thought he'd burst! Floodlights still on, shutters still open, crazy old men out in storm, finding corpses—I thought he was going to throw himself down and drum his heels on the floor. He's calmed down now, I suppose. You'll be able to see for yourself, because I've got orders to tell him the moment you come to, so that he can pass the word on to your other friends."

"Uh?"

"Police, stupid. They're wild! I'm going to make a chart of your contusions, so I can prove if they start roughing you up. One out in the passage all the time. 'Smorning he tried to pinch my bum, so next time I came past I sort of tripped and spilled old Turnbull's bed-pan over him. Only they'd changed shifts and I got the wrong one. What'll I tell Follicle?"

"I'm tired."

"Of course you are, but . . . See how you're feeling after lunch, shall I? Manage an egg?"

"Urrh."

"I'm sure you can."

He let her take his pulse then lay with closed eyes and listened to her moving around the room, adjusting the robot, humming as she worked. Never again, he thought. Never another chance. All your working life you are vaguely conscious of the coming shadow. Not me, you say. I won't be like that. I'd sooner be dead. But as if by one of those mathematical niceties at which nature is so adept, your will declines just faintly ahead of your body and mind. You can never quite bring yourself to do it. Only if, like Pibble, you have been most of the way down that dreary incline, and then miraculously hauled back, does the equation briefly reverse its sign. Now you can do it, pat. Now, before the downward slither begins anew . . . for Pibble, that *now* had been the night of the storm, and would not come again.

It was Jenny who had performed the miracle, Jenny whom, therefore, he had let down by failing to take his chance. The determination formed in his mind that he would not tell her why he had gone out and climbed the tower. The resolve seemed as firm as its motives were feeble. Vaguely he told himself that she would be hurt, that she wouldn't understand . . . but at the same time he knew that part of his plan had assumed that if he had brought it off, then she would have understood . . .

Though it was clear now that the dream had not been a dream, it still seemed as if its reality was only maintained by the reality of her presence. As soon as she closed the door what had been certain began to blur and shift once more. A man's voice spoke in the passage and hers answered, sharp as a green lemon. He ached. That was real. Jenny was real. Everything else . . . wait . . . the man in the passage . . . she'd answered him, thus making *him* real . . . if he was still there . . . just got to get up and see . . .

He started to rise, but his head was only six inches from the pillow when the darkness came suddenly down, roaring.

She woke him with lunch, and insisted on feeding him eggy mush, morsel by morsel, nurse and nothing else. She spoke little, he not at all. The plan had not allowed for failure; he realised now that he hadn't dared to imagine what she would think, say, do . . . How the relationship might wither. She picked up an invalid cup and held the spout to his lips. He sucked. It was Guinness. A dribble of hope.

"That's nice," he said. "Thank you."

"Doctor Follick will be here in five minutes."

Not even the nickname.

"What are you going to tell him?"

"Don't know."

"Please."

For the first time her eyes really met his, green in her flattish pale face. Normally there was a faint cast in her left eye, a sign of her being relaxed and cheerful. It wasn't there now. She bit her lip, thinking.

"You're going to have to mind your step," she said. "Follicle's very in with the shareholders. Remember, we're really run for their benefit, so that they can have somewhere comfy to go when they get old, so however frightful they are we can't get rid of them once they're here. That means all the rest of the residents—people like you—have to be extra amenable, to make up. If Follicle tells the shareholders that somebody's a disruptive influence, then they

29

have to go, no matter how much they're paying. So you see—
you'll have to think of something. If you don't tell me what it is, I
shan't be able to back you up, shall I?"

"Don't know."

Her sigh was almost a snort as she turned from the bed,
whisking the tray away in the same moment. Why the vehemence,
the urgency? Doddering out one night, though a nuisance, hardly
counted as disruption, surely. Doddering out, deliberately, to die,
though . . . He couldn't keep his mind engaged at all with the main
question—what to say to Follick? It slithered around like a drill-
point sidling away from the marked spot on a surface too hard for
it, now here, now there, and then suddenly biting into the softer
stuff of memory. *A ward, fifty yards long, six inches between the
huddled beds. The stench of age battling with the reek of disinfec-
tants, and winning—an odour worse than any zoo. A particular
pillow, the large grey face on it creased with perpetual weeping. The
little Chinese doctor saying quietly and with no sign of surprise that
the man was undoubtedly senile now, irrecoverably helpless. Greasy
Jack Phillipps, grandfather of fences, who with all his wits about
him three months before had decided this would be a cunning place
to hide when the Great Christie's Raid went haywire . . .*

Fingers touched his wrist—not hers, but strong, dry, electric.
He opened his eyes to see Toby Follick's face floating above him.

Pibble liked Doctor Follick. When, after the Hackney disaster,
his normal perceptions had begun to return, enabling him gradually to become aware of the inappropriate opulence in which
Thanassi Thanatos's random generosity had plumped him down,
this liking had been one of the first excuses he had made to himself
for staying on at Flycatchers. He was used to the masks of
doctors. During the course of his working life he had come to
approve of a mild level of charlatanism in those he had
interviewed—doctors whose patients had disappeared, or done
their wives in, or themselves, or had invented more ingeniously
anti-social forms of dottiness. With experience he had come to
believe that even the most fraudulent-seeming might be good at

30

his job, and not despite the fraud but because of it. Then private experience had reinforced this belief. Pibble had chosen his own doctor, a jovial, lazy Greek, on the grounds that this one at least made no pretence at being anything more than a pretty moderate sort of healer. He had found too late that even this mild incompetence was a mask—Doctor Palagoutis had been a much worse doctor than he'd pretended. After such a man has failed to diagnose your wife's illness before it is terminal, you are less impressed by apparent openness and cynicism, more prepared to tolerate the masks of scientist or country squire or priest—or, in the case of Toby Follick, comic conjurer.

"Well, well, well," murmured Follick, in tones of pleased surprise. The doggy brown eyes glistened with interest, as though Pibble was a rabbit which had popped out of the wrong hat.

Flycatchers' resident physician was a neat little man. There was no good reason, apart from his name, for Jenny's calling him Follicle. He was not conspicuously hairy nor shiny-bald, but his hair was greying and receding tactfully in keeping with his age. For all that, the nickname worked, drawing attention to something intangibly odd in his appearance. Pibble had come to the conclusion that his head was a little too large for his body, perhaps at any rate it somehow added to the whole effect of an otherwise precise and sober middle-aged doctor exuding this happy experimental eagerness of a fourteen-year-old boy.

"Been a nuisance. Sorry," mumbled Pibble.

"Far from it. Example to us all. How are you feeling?"

"A bit sore."

"No wonder. Jenny, where's the holy book?"

Jenny moved for a moment into Pibble's sphere of vision, carrying the morocco-bound, gold-tooled folder in which patients' charts were kept at Flycatchers. She was not quite comfortable with Follick's manner, and this came out in an extra starchiness in her own. Follick studied the documents with care.

"Interesting," he said. "I wonder . . . Let's haruspicate a bit. Off with the altar-cloths, Jenny."

The medical rites continued, always with that slight element of parody throughout the proddings and peerings. Follick handled his stethoscope, for instance, not as though he actually expected it to turn into a snake, but as though he'd know what to do, supposing it did. He seemed to be unusually thorough, but at last he straightened and stood aside, letting Jenny restore the authentic ritual by covering up the sacrificial animal.

"You're in remarkably good nick," said Follick. "You ought to have killed yourself, you know."

"Yes," said Pibble, more firmly than he meant to.

"But you didn't, and that makes me think . . . there's something I'd like to . . . Is he due for a surgery visit this week, Jenny?"

"No."

"Fix one with Maisie, will you? Give him a couple of days to pick up strength—longer if he needs it; you might find he has a bit of a low tomorrow . . . And we can do without that doofer now."

He waved a dismissive arm towards the gadget by the bed. There was a curious moment of emptiness, everyone waiting for everyone else.

"You might as well take it down straight away," said Follick.

"Alan locks the store at eleven and has his break."

"That still gives you ten minutes."

Without waiting for an answer Follick turned and strolled to the window, where he stood looking out, bathed in the wintry light. His coat was a snowdrift crisped with frost, out of which his head poked with the stunned but lively air of a skier who has just taken a huge but painless tumble. Pibble hardly noticed him because Jenny, as she unstrapped his arm and peeled the cable from the crook of his elbow, was having one of her rages, those controlled internal storms which she refused to let ruffle her surface, refused even to admit she had had but which could be triggered off by incidents which would not have bothered anyone else. She eased the plaster painlessly from his skin, but he could feel her fury as if it had been an audible throb. She avoided his eye until she had to back to wheel the robot through the door. He

32

winked. Now she let the rage flash from her eyes, and was gone. Follick turned as though the whuffle of the closing door was the signal he'd been waiting for.

"The cops are after you, James."

"Ur."

"We've been fending them off."

"I'd better see them."

"It's not as easy as that. You've had a near thing, you know. If Sankey hadn't been out looking for Tosca . . ."

"Ur?"

"One of the night security men, bloke called Tosca, was missing. What's more he hadn't turned off the floodlights or closed the security shutters; he was supposed to do that from a couple of switches in the kitchen—first the shutters, then nip round and check they'd all closed, then the floodlighting . . ."

Of course. The footsteps. The two big switches. The lights.

". . . But he hadn't. You know what this place is like for strict routine. Sankey went out to look for him at his watch-post, which was a room in the water-tower. Halfway to the tower Sankey found you crawling towards the house, apparently delirious, and gabbling about a body on the roof."

"I don't remember any of that."

"No?"

"It was there, though?"

"The body? Yes. Sankey got you in and handed you over to Jenny. You were unconscious by then. That's what I mean—you wouldn't actually have made it back to the front door. Now . . ."

"Bullet wound?"

"So I gather. They're being extremely close about it. That's not the point. What I'm trying to get into your head is that you've had a close call. You've been gaga for a couple of days, and now you've surfaced, but I wouldn't be surprised if you went gaga again tomorrow. You're in shock, and with your rotten blood-pressure . . . Listen, I've got a responsibility to the cops, of course, but in my book I've got a bigger one to you. I've got to tell them

33

whether you're up to answering questions. From their point of
view that means whether you'll pass out before they've finished
with you, but from mine it means whether being questioned is
going to set you back, and if so how much. Understand?"

"Ur."

"Well, I can't see how I'm expected to make an estimate on
something like that until I know what form the interview's likely
to take. How much stress it will involve. Uh? They aren't telling
me a thing, so the only person I can ask is you. Uh?"

"Ur."

"So I suppose the first question is how much can you remember?"

"I'm not sure. I get muddled."

(A half-truth. The events of the storm night, though dream-like
in their patches of clarity—the ghost in the mirror, the swirling
away of hat and body, the strange warmth of the tower room—
still pieced together with very little of the blurred transitions of
dream. But Pibble felt prickly with the almost superstitious fear of
admitting anything, a feeling that old lags share with the ordinary
old, because anything you say may be used against you.)

"Don't we all?" said Follick, acknowledging a cliché of life at
Flycatchers. "But I'd have said you're more on the spot than
most, and getting better all the time. You didn't just get up and
potter out on a dopy way—I mean you got dressed. You made a
dummy. You can remember doing that?"

"I suppose so."

"Then I'd have thought you ought to be able to remember *why*
you did it."

His tone was only puzzled and friendly, but suddenly Pibble felt
hunted. The mysterious shareholders, the ultimate source of
authority at Flycatchers . . . their passion for routine and
smoothness . . . the vision of Greasy Jack, weeping in his geriatric
hell . . .

"I heard a shot," he said.

"What!"

"Learn to know the sound."

"Yes, of course, but . . ."

Follick looked utterly baffled, but not at all disbelieving. He was an expert himself, and so more easily convinced by other realms of expertise. Can't tell him, thought Pibble. He'd have to pass it on. Tell the police and ask them not to . . .

"But the storm!"

"Came and went. Heard it in a lull. Unmistakable."

"But . . ."

"Just after Jenny finished. Didn't want her to worry. Didn't want anyone to worry. Got up and dressed. Left the bathroom door open while I was doing that—make it look as if I was in the bathroom. Couldn't ask anyone else to go and look, you see—stupid old fool, you know . . . made the dummy because Jenny would be coming back and she'd know I'd just been to the bathroom . . . had to go and see. Wouldn't have slept at all."

Follick nodded, frowning. A better explanation might have impressed him less—he was used to the old. He stood for a while rocking from toe to heel and back, like one of those bar-room toys that endlessly teeters to its point of balance and returns.

"See them soon as they like," said Pibble. "If I'm going to have a low tomorrow . . ."

"I only said you might."

"This afternoon. Have a rest now. Four o'clock?"

"I've got to go to town. Can't get out of it. It's a Sultan's mother-in-law."

"I'll be all right."

"I'll see that Jenny's here, though."

"No," murmured Pibble. "No."

It was the last thing he wanted, but he couldn't make his voice produce more than a flutter of opposition. Boredom was floating down on him in the familiar grey softness, burying him helpless in its drift. He drew it to him, snuggled into it, making it his shelter against the hard-edged world. He was so ill, so old. They oughtn't to . . .

35

"Tried to sit up," he sighed. "Only a little. Blacked out."

Follick nodded. This collapse of will was as common a symptom as any among his patients.

"I can tell them you still aren't up to it," he said. "Put it off till I can be there."

"No."

Not that either. Nothing. What was the use? All along, all through his struggle, the Liberator had been already dead.

He lay still, wavering in and out of doze. Jenny must have come in while he was below the surface of sleep because he woke and knew she was there by the quiet flip of a page. She had taken to spending her rest-hour in his chair, reading; sword-and-sorcery, SF, a few thrillers. Tolkien apart she despised most of what she read but refused to try anything else because what she called "proper books" only made her miserable. He had become used to her presence, a silent element like a pool or tree beside which he drowsed, but this afternoon he slowly perceived that the nature of that presence had altered. It was as though the tree was full of flies, or the pool smelt strange.

"What's the time?" he whispered.

"Ten past three. Go back to sleep. You've got nearly an hour still."

"You don't have to stay."

"I'm staying."

"But . . ."

"Follicle hoofed me out so that he could talk to you alone. I'm not having you doing it too."

"I'll be all right."

"Of course you will. I've seen them. They're better than I'd expected—one of them knows you."

But he was already burrowing back into the grey drift and could only produce the vaguest gargle of dissent. If Jenny stayed . . . Will flailed, trying to grapple Mind to its duty, but Mind was away, ducking through the maze of corridors that riddled the ruined

36

palace of memory. Sometimes, like flashes from the outer day, imagined snatches of the coming interview might obtrude, but Mind shied from them, back into the shadows . . . *A bedside, a bleak single ward, the body on the bed bandaged like a mummy, one eye and the lower face still visible. That eye bright and fierce with will, and the mouth clamped shut, so tight that it seemed to be munching its own lips. Not one word out of her till she died, though it had been an open-and-shut case anyway. Her own son, twenty-nine stab wounds, squabble over a van-load of stolen knitwear . . .* Heard a shot? In that wind? Come off it . . . *Addressing myself now to the prisoner Foyle. I single you out, Foyle, from these evil men because, strange though it may seem, your wickedness is greater than theirs. True, they have done many things that were individually vile. Murder, robbery, extortion, prostitution, drug peddling—these are crimes against society as well as against the individual victims of those crimes. But you, Foyle, as a senior and respected police officer, the supposed guardian of society, have committed a greater crime. You have poisoned the wells of justice. Justice is the mortar of our society. Without it the fabric will not stand. It is for this reason that, in a very real sense, the smallest lie by a police officer must be considered a more serious offence than the greatest crime by a private citizen . . .* OK, let's say there was a lull, and you heard it and decided to go and look. It was dark. It's a big garden. High up? I see these windows are double glazed . . . *And here, gentlemen, punctual as the Flying Scot, you can observe rigor beginning to set in. The jaw is already almost too stiff for me to, ngff, come on my beauty don't be coy, there, force open and the neck muscles are showing the same symptoms of protein precipitation . . .*

"Jenny?"

"I'm staying, and that's flat. I want to know what's going on."

. . . Helpless. You start helpless. Slowly you conquer a kingdom, impose your will, first on your own body, then on your surroundings, then on other people. But the kingdom shrinks. The frontier moves in. No other people in it, only objects your subjects. Then not even those, not your own body . . . *large room, crammed with furniture, dust on the glistening veneers. Persian rugs on walls. Blue line painted on floor, dividing room. Thick oil paint, three inches wide, slap across good carpet. At one end little old woman lying on Madame Recamier day-bed, mouth open, flies, dead five days. Brother (smoking jacket, prince-nez) reading* Telegraph *other end of room. "Nothing to do with me—that's her side." Gestures at blue frontier, goes back to paper* . . . Not my body. Rupert of Hentzau.

He must have genuinely slept. A figure in glossy black boots, frilled shirt open to the navel, came and went, not always the same face but always handsome as the devil, laughing like the devil before turning away to display a mess of hair and bone and brain at the back of the head.

Jenny woke him with a touch on his cheek and he opened his eyes to see her wearing her starched uniform cap, nurse at her nursest.

"The gentlemen have come to talk to you," she said. "Do you feel up to it?"

"Urrgh."

"Want a pee before they come?"

"I'm all right."

"I think you'd better. You don't want . . . ."

He gave in. She needed to demonstrate her power, not to him, but to them. Keep them waiting. When he'd done she took the bottle to the bathroom, returned, wiped the crust of sleep-spittle from the corner of his mouth, straightened his sheets and at last went to the door and muttered. Two men came quietly into the room—one big and one small but both as surely policemen to Pibble as a dog is a dog to another dog, however human breeders may have reshaped them. The small man wore his black hair almost to his shoulders, which made his thin face seem even thinner and paler than it really was. He looked a little over thirty. The large man must have been twenty years older—heavy, balding but not bothered about it, pale eyes set wide in the many-seamed face.

"'Lo, Jimmy," said the large man. "Good to see you again."

38

Pibble felt his brow pucker even while he was forcing his lips into a smile of fake recognition. The past was too much with him. Readable emotions crossed the large man's face, the welcome suffused with mild hurt at not being known, and discomfort at the sight of the creature lying on the bed. Behind these, less readable, lay a sense of doubt. Pibble spoke on a note of query that sounded more like complaint.

"Mike Crewe?"

"Got it," said the large man, almost in the same breath.

"But I thought—weren't you Chief Super, last I heard?"

"For my sins," said Mike, smug in his mock sadness.

"Det-super Cass," he added, nodding at the other man. "Ted to his friends. Ted's running the case—I'm just taking the excuse to come and say hello. Ted, this is my old boss, Jimmy Pibble."

"Hi," said Cass with a wary smile. Iago to Crewe's extrovert Moor. Awkward relationship for him, big gun on his manor, one witness big gun's old crony. "The doctor says we mustn't stay more than ten mins."

"See how it goes," said Pibble. "Jenny will blow the whistle."

Neither man glanced at her, but a signal seemed to pass. Crewe settled into the visitor's chair. Cass pulled the other one up to the bed and perched on its arm, in a pose of curious tension which made him look as though he were poised an inch above it, like a frame from a film of a man in the act of springing up. He leaned forward.

"We'll cut the corners and save time," he said. "This is just prelim. And you know the form, of course. Now, deceased was George Tosca, employed here as security guard with some other duties. Body found on top of water-tower, two shots in back of head, close range. Death instant, around eight forty-five, give or take half an hour. Soon after death, but long enough for blood to begin drying, body turned over to lie on its back. Body discovered at ten fifty-two by Sankey, the night porter, following up remarks made by you. Right?"

"I don't remember talking to Sankey."

"But finding the body?"

39

"I suppose so. Dressed like an actor?"

"That's right. Did you touch it?"

"I moved his arm. Before I knew what it was."

"You didn't turn him over?"

Pibble could only shake his head, letting the gesture indicate how far from possible such an effort would have been.

"Lying on his back?" insisted Cass.

"Ur."

"You didn't see the weapon?"

"No. Where . . ."

"On the far side of the body—tucked under him, almost. Somebody wearing knitted gloves had wiped it and put it there. Size of hand unknown—we were lucky to get the knitting. See anything else?"

"Don't know. Fairly beat up by then—climbing, you know. My legs aren't . . . Wasn't there a room? Up. Second floor? A long garden chair. Something on the floor—I thought it was a snake, but I suppose . . ."

"His holster. Black leather, with cross-belt. He'd put a lot of polishing into it, but it only had his own prints."

". . . And a paraffin stove, was it? I didn't see the stove, but I think I smelt it."

Mike Crewe answered, carefully toneless.

"He'd made himself comfortable, Jimmy. He was supposed to be guarding that side of the main building. He'd been issued with a loud hailer and a high-powered rifle, as well as his hand-gun. But he'd made himself comfortable. Chair to lie down in, radio, paraffin heaters. The window was shut and misted up on the inside, too."

"All those guns?"

"Licenses quite in order. Special permission."

"He must have been something special himself, then," said Pibble.

"Not really," said Mike, still non-committal. "He came here with one of the residents—job-description chauffeur, but more

40

like a bodyguard. Flycatchers is used to that sort of set-up, so they took him on to the security staff. Only he doesn't seem to have taken his duties very seriously."

"He did his rounds very regularly," said Pibble. "You could set your watch by him."

"How do you know?" said Cass, just managing not to pounce.

"I'm right above the kitchen door. I used to hear him coming and going."

"But not on Thursday night," said Cass.

"I mightn't have heard. There was a storm."

"There was too," said Cass, softly.

A brief pause, as though that section of the interview had ended and they were about to move on to fresh ground. But Pibble recognised the moment well—he had used it himself, often. You let the chappie relax, think he's clear, and then you punch him. It was surprising how well his own wits seemed to be working, as though the policemen's presence—Mike's in particular—was restorative, forcing him to square moral shoulders, pull up moral socks, not be seen in a state of total dissolution, though he might well have to take refuge in that state, because this surge of energies had brought him to another decision. With Jenny in the room he was going to stick to his lie. It shouldn't do much damage. He'd be bound to be able to see Mike alone before long and tell him the truth. It wasn't the sort of thing anyway which pushes a case along the wrong tracks—an old buffer who thought he heard a shot . . .

"Yes," said Cass quietly. "It was quite a storm. But Doctor Follick tells me you heard a shot. He says you were quite definite about it."

"Well . . . yes, I suppose I was sure at the time. It was just after Jenny left me. Between nine twenty-five and nine thirty, then. There was a lull in the storm, and I heard it—knew what it was at once. *Thought* I knew, I mean. If you asked me now . . . Anyway, I lay there for a minute or two, and then I started to get in a fret . . . when you get old, you know . . ."

"You're sixty-four, Jimmy," said Mike rather sharply. "I

41

looked you up."

"I know, I know. It's blood-pressure . . . has the same effect . . . Jenny will tell you . . ."

"He's perfectly all right," said Jenny in a dry voice. "He's good for years and years. But he's been very ill, and that's like being old. Go on. You haven't got much longer."

"I'm all right," said Pibble. "Listen, I told you about the man who came to the kitchen door to do the shutters and the lights. I didn't know his name was Tosca, but I guessed he must be one of the security men. I thought I'd just go down and tell him about the shot. I got up and dressed . . ."

"Why?" interrupted Cass. (Not *How?*—he wouldn't see that that was the real question. Jenny would, though.)

"Keep warm. I get cold, you know . . . besides, this man, finding some old idiot in the kitchen, still in his dressing-gown, rabbitting on about hearing a shot . . ."

Mike grunted affirmation. He was a good policeman. He understood about the obstinate vanity of decay—old women spending half an hour putting on their make-up before tottering along to the station to report some urgent horror, old men . . .

"You made a dummy," said Cass.

"I didn't want Jenny to worry."

They glanced at her for confirmation.

"He didn't want me to find out, more likely," she said, still remote and clinical. "Then he could tease me about it next morning. It's a game, you know. They like doing things they're not supposed to, just to show they still can."

"Some Colditz!" said Cass. "Where were you while all this was going on, me old Stalagführer?"

"Putting my other patients to bed, I imagine."

"You were in Turnbull's room when I went by," said Pibble.

"You couldn't have . . . oh, yes, that's right—I went back to him."

"OK," said Cass with a reluctant shrug. "So you went down to the kitchen to wait for Tosca. But he didn't come. Because he was dead. Then . . .?"

"I'm not quite sure. I suppose getting down there had taken it out of me a bit more than I expected. Perhaps I was feeling a bit cocky about having got that far. I got impatient. I went and tried the door—I expected it to be locked, you see, but it wasn't—"

"You're quite sure about that?" interrupted Cass.

"Oh, yes. How else could I have got out, otherwise?"

"They run this place like a fortress," said Crewe. "Everything locked. That's right, isn't it, Nurse?"

"Yes," said Jenny. "I mean, we've got our own door in the staff wing, but we aren't allowed night keys to it. It's always locked just before dark, and after that we have to come in and out through the main entrance."

"OK, I'll check what the routine was for the kitchen door," said Cass.

"Somebody usually saw the kitchen staff out after supper and locked it," said Pibble. "I could hear them, but the storm . . ."

"Right," said Cass. "But at any rate it was unlocked around ten o'clock. You opened the door, and then . . ."

"Well, I went out," said Pibble. "I don't know why—it seems perfectly stupid now. I suppose the storm mightn't have been so bad in the courtyard, and I'd got it into my head I wanted to find the chap, and then . . . Well, the door blew shut, for a start, so I couldn't get back in that way. Had to get round to the front. Started off and . . . fell over. Wind, it was like . . . anyway started crawling, I suppose, and just went on. Stupid. Found myself at the tower—must have gone wrong way, you know. Wind. Door open, went inside for shelter—at least that's what must have happened. I can't remember *deciding* to do any of these things. Expect I crawled across and sat on the bottom step—remember feeling I couldn't just sit there. I'd better do something. Started to climb up. Habit, you know."

"Habit?"

"You tell them, Jenny."

"I think we'd better stop soon," said Jenny. "Can you hear how

43

tired he's getting?"

"I'm all right," said Pibble, aware that he had been overdoing the note of feebleness in order to force them to accept his story. "Give me a bit of a rest. Tell them about stairs."

He closed his eyes and half-listened to Jenny's explanation. His body seemed detached from his mind, the former whining with aches and weariness, the latter eager as a puppy on a walk. Even if he hadn't had a position to defend, a need for alertness, he might have had something of the same feeling. It was as though the working machinery of investigation—Mike and Cass—carried a voltage strong enough to wake inductive currents in his discarded circuits.

"Well, I suppose it's pleasant to have a couple of mysteries cleared up," said Mike.

"If you say so," said Cass, mock-subservient. "I'll check with the kitchen staff about the door—now I come to think of it, there was something about that first time through . . ."

(Rustle of notebook leaves.)

"Yes. I've only put a query. I remember now. One of them—the fat one—wanted to say something and the thin one interrupted her. Damn. I should have gone back to that earlier . . . What else? This shot, if that's what it was . . ."

"Just one," whispered Pibble, eyes still closed. "Didn't hear the other one."

"A little after nine twenty-five . . . that's ten minutes beyond the pathologist's outer limit."

"I wouldn't worry about that, Ted," said Mike. "A different boffin would have given you a different limit. Bloody cold night, wasn't it? Snow thawing with the body-warmth, adding to the wind-chill . . . How old is this boffin?"

"Youngish. Nobody's made him a knight yet."

"There. If he'd been a bit older he'd have allowed himself double the lee-way."

Pibble, eyes still closed, was aware of a tautness between the two men, an unspoken area of dispute, reaching beyond the timing of the shot. It relieved itself in movement. Cass's voice came from near the window.

"That's a fine old cedar out there," he said. "I've heard a tree like that make some pretty odd noises in a storm."

"It groans," said Jenny. "I've never heard it bang."

"Dendrophonics *and* medicine," said Cass.

Pibble sensed the conversation floating beyond his reach. Jenny's sudden, firm intrusion, as if determined that *her* patient must be a reliable witness . . . Cass's instinct to tease her . . . a nip of jealousy . . .

"It could have been the cedar," he said, loudly. "I thought of it at the time and decided it wasn't."

"Let's leave it at that," said Mike.

There were sounds of rising. Pibble opened his eyes and saw him standing by the bed, smiling down.

"We'll leave you alone now, Jimmy . . ."

"A couple of mysteries?"

"What? Oh yes. The tower stairs. I don't know whether you noticed when you were doing your circus act, but they didn't get cleaned very often. Plenty of dust, just right for footprints. Policeman's dream. Only somebody had worked the whole way up, sweeping them clean all down the middle where the prints would have been. Gun wiped, we thought. Stairs swept clean. Rummy bit of work . . . We weren't to know, were we, that an old friend had gone slithering up on his arse wiping all those prints out?"

"Crippen! I'm sorry, Mike."

"Not your fault, mate. And Tosca had swept his hidey-hole out, so that wasn't any good either."

"I'm sorry."

"Forget it, Jimmy. I mean, it would have been handy to have some prints, but at least we're better off than we were, trying to work out how our chappie had the nerve to spend the time doing that job."

"And who'd have thought it necessary," said Cass. "We don't

have half a million footprints on computer, do we?"

Pibble lay staring up at Crewe, stunned with guilt. The sense of alertness, of being at least mentally his old self, was sucked away like water down a drain. He had the impulse, as the last swirls vanished, to blurt out his real reasons for climbing the tower, to atone for this huge mess by undoing his minor lie; but before he could grasp at the notion all will had gurgled away.

"Don't worry, Jimmy," said Mike in a changed voice. "I shouldn't have told you. Worse things happen every day, remember?"

"I'm sorry," seemed to be all Pibble's lips would say.

"I think you'd better go now," said Jenny, her voice for the first time tinged with something more than medical dispassion.

"Right. Come along, Ted. See you, Jimmy."

"Come and see me again," whispered Pibble.

They were gone.

Come and see me again. I can tell you then. Come and see me alone. Old days. Like the old days. Never come back. Come back . . .

He felt Jenny's hand at his pulse.

"Are you all right, Jimmy?"

She wouldn't understand. It was no use. For the moment she represented only the world of sickness and helplessness which for a while he seemed to have escaped.

"Just tired," he whispered. "I'm all right."

"Do you think you can go back to sleep for a bit?"

"Urrh."

She stood for a moment, then smoothed his bedclothes and moved away. Through the sigh of the door he heard the mutter of male voices. Before they could wake in him fresh springs of guilt he pulled sleep down over himself and hid.

While he slept a decision made itself. It was quite easy. There were writing things in his bedside table. There was a police guard in the corridor. He could write a note to Mike—two short

46

sentences to explain that he had heard no shot, but that the rest of the story was true, and a third to say he didn't want the staff at Flycatchers to know. Weak though he was, he could surely reach the man in the corridor, some time when Jenny's routine took her elsewhere . . .

He woke decisively, almost as though the train of thought had been a coherent one, despite being the product of sleep. He was already moving his arm out from the bedclothes to reach for pen and paper when he saw that she was in the room, sitting quietly in one of the chairs, watching him.

"I think you're marvellous," she said.

"Oh?"

He was confused, and thought she must be talking about the note he was preparing to write.

"Your friend thinks so too."

"Uh?"

"They were still out in the passage when I left you, talking about what you'd said. The thin one must have been saying something about not believing you, because your friend—he wasn't angry, but he was very serious—telling him that if you said it it was true. He saw me coming and asked me to back him up, so of course I did. Then they moved off. I listened as long as I could, but it wasn't very much. He was starting to tell the other man about some case you'd once been in—someone called Smith, was it?"

"The Smith Machine. Mike's too young."

"He said it was before his time. I didn't hear any more. What was it about, Jimmy?"

"My boss was bent. The Smith brothers had bought him. I was the chief witness."

"That must have been awful for you!"

(Typical. Despite her air of having grown and come to flower in some garden untouched by the rots or aphids of the ordinary world, she knew what mattered.)

"Yes. Don't let's talk about it."

47

"All right. Perhaps you'd better not talk at all."

"I'm all right. Had a good sleep. Wasn't quite so done up as I made out."

"I thought you were bright as a button till right at the end. You liked having them here, didn't you?"

"I suppose so."

"I was glad the Follicle had to go and see his Sultan. It was very interesting—though I don't suppose a real interrogation's like that."

"Haven't they interrogated all the staff?"

"Oh, yes. Just asking where we were—that sort of thing. Whether we knew George Tosca, and so on."

"Did you?"

"A bit—you couldn't really help it. He was . . . oh, suppose you were new here, he'd manage to be hanging around when you arrived, take your case up for you, all gallant, make sure you spotted he had a pass-key . . ."

She was talking flippantly, but her voice had an uncharacteristic dryness.

"Did he have much luck?" said Pibble.

"I shouldn't wonder . . . It can't have left him a lot of time for bodyguarding, anyway. I wish I knew why Mr X needed a bodyguard."

"What makes you think . . ."

"Well, it's obvious, isn't it?"

"Did they arrive together? Tosca was somebody's chauffeur, Mike said. Did he take Wilson out for drives?"

"That's not his real name. Why won't you call him Mr X?"

"Because I'm old and stupid and if I met him I might call him the wrong thing."

"You aren't stupid and you aren't old. Anyway, no, not much. Mr X never goes out of his room, and I don't think George came up and saw him much—but listen, now I remember, about three months ago the shareholders ordered a blitz on security. They had all the locks changed, and made new rules about keys, and—this is

48

the point—they hired an extra security man, and it was George. And just after that Mr X came."

"So they didn't come together."

"No, but if Mr X wanted special extra security, he might want it to be a secret too, mightn't he? He might have got them to do it that way so that nobody'd realise it was being done for him."

"It's possible, but . . ."

"Don't you see, that would explain why George was shot. So that whoever it is Mr X is hiding from could get at him."

It was a game, a new toy that really amused her. The horror of killing seemed scarcely to touch her.

"A professional hit-man would have brought his own gun," he said.

"Oh! But . . . Look, he could have held George up with his own gun, taken George's from him and shot him with that, couldn't he?"

"Why was Tosca wearing that rig?"

"Because he was the vainest man I ever met, that's why."

"Was there a mirror in the room?"

"No . . . at least I don't imagine there was. Why?"

"Because vain men like to be seen, if only by themselves, when they are all dressed up. I think it's much more likely he dressed up *for* somebody."

"What do you mean?"

"If he was the sort of man you say he was—rabbitting after the nurses all the time—much the most likely explanation is that he'd dressed up for one of them."

"But that's the whole point. We were all locked in from six o'clock, for a start, and by the time you heard the shot we were all up to our necks in work, putting patients to bed."

"I didn't mean . . . it doesn't have to be . . ."

"Who else is there? Mrs Foyle goes home, and so do the cleaners except for Mrs Finsky and Mrs O'Hara. They'd knocked off early to watch Kevin O'Hara on telly in the Cup re-play. Anybody from outside would have to get Mr Finsky to open the main gate, or else climb the fence and come up through the woods. I can just about see some dopy girl doing that for George, but it's much more likely to be some thug who actually came to kill him."

"You said he had pass-keys. He could have given . . ."

"Oh, honestly! I wish you'd use all this cleverness on Mr X! If only you'd met him you'd see it had to be something to do with him!"

"It isn't a game, my dear."

"It is. And you're an old spoilsport," she said, bouncing out of her chair to glare down at him. She was acting out her irritation, hamming it up, but he was aware of a core of genuine anger. The idea of somebody she knew and worked with being Tosca's lover and then Tosca's murderer was too close to the grimy world for her; an actual passion binding tangible people in the charmless linkage of cause and effect. She wanted to shift the story into her imagined world of latter-day orcs and dragons, where Mr X belonged. No doubt this was one of the things that fed their affection for each other—despite his own helplessness he was still able to feel protective towards her, and she to rely on him. He smiled, and she accepted the peace-offering.

"Well you're not going to blame it on me," she said. "I was washing my hair at half past eight, and Maisie was helping me, so there!"

"Good," he said. "It's a help to be able to cross a few suspects off."

She laughed, bent, and kissed him. She was still laughing as she left the room. He lay still, concentrating as usual on the residual feel of her kiss, willing the imprint to last—dryish, snow soft and tingling as snow might, but warm with energy. Too fast it faded, dwindling like an image held in the retina under closed eyelids, gone. With it seemed to vanish the moral energy with which he had woken. The spectres of gibberish came flickering out of the marshes, no longer kept at bay by intellectual fires—tedious, inane, repetitive, the Frenchman, the boiler-house, Teal's slate . . .

Irritably he blew on the embers. All that happened was a small flare, the memory of her kiss. But changed. Icy, quick, almost rubbery, cold fire. *Ice cream for supper? Once a detective always a detective. A mess, glistening on his spread hand, a taste in his mouth, raspberry jam and suet duff, licked from his thumb in the dark niche of the scullery.* The muscles of his heart clenched like a fist. Somebody groaned. The fist unclenched with a clumsy double-bump as he forced his head and shoulders up from the pillows, and then the darkness came roaring down.

Three

A BAD TIME followed, repeating a pattern from earlier in his illness. The self would gather towards the daylight, like a crew on shore leave stumbling out of stews and taverns to assemble, hung-over and feverish, on the grimy quays of the conscious world; only then, when almost fully gathered into the waking self, would they observe that the harbour was weirdly different from the one in which they had anchored the evening before, and know that their ship, lying dark on the dawn water, still carried night in its hold. The world to which he seemed to have woken was no more real than the one he had left.

This could happen many times in sequence. Each time he had to take the ensuing dream for reality until the illusion withered with the next fake waking. By the time reality truly dawned, half the crew would be mutinous and refuse to accept the sunrise as anything except another false dawn. Such days would end in a mess of memories, any of which seemed as true, or false, as any of the others. Walking along a sea-shore, looking for a surgeon, because a large flat limpet had clamped itself to the side of his mouth, irremovable. Waking from that horror to remember that the doctors had stuck a dressing there and when it was peeled away the skin beneath would be a patch of young flesh, a beginning of renewal. Drowsing up into another layer to understand that he had as usual been dribbling in his sleep and the saliva had dried. In the layer beyond that trying to shave, seeing himself in the mirror, a leper, the lion face . . .

Sometimes Jenny was there, feeding him small mouthfuls or coaxing drink between his lips or taking his pulse or helping him piss—or simply there, sitting in her usual chair. With one element of his mind he knew that if she was there then he was awake, because he never dreamed about her; but with another element he was aware that her presence was the fore-runner of a nightmare, to which even the horrors of the limpet and the lion face were preferable. This was something permanent, and in a vague way he understood that he was going to have to face it, that the process of escape by surrender to the world of dream could not go on for ever, because in fact his body was steadily recovering from the exhaustion of Thursday night, and that sooner or later it would force him to have a "good" day, and then the nightmare would become real.

The good day began much like the bad, with waking, being cleaned by somebody not Jenny, swallowing food, slithering back into the shifting smother of self-induced delirium. There was a presence in the room, a total stranger in a dressing-gown, who became Dickie Foyle, who became a shadowy and nameless schoolmaster, who became the stranger in the dressing-gown again . . .

"Didn't wake you, did I?"

"Urrugh?"

"Just thought I'd take a look at you, see?"

The sense of reality was very solid. He began to accept it. Even the most disaffected of the crew shrugged and readied for a voyage.

"Course, I know a bit about you long before," said the slow, leaden voice. The stranger was squat and elderly. His yellowish face seemed to be partly moulded of not very convincing flesh-toned Plasticine. His dressing-gown was quilted green and he wore it over mauve silk pyjamas. He shuffled nearer the bed and gazed down. His eyes were small and pale, set wide apart under

53

barely visible brows. The yellow of his scalp was mottled and veined; close-cropped grey hair covered the sides of his head. The Plasticine look was of course real flesh, flesh which had once been all jowl and pink pudge, now wasted. His lips were mauve, the lower one twisted at one side into a heavy pad. Waking or sleeping, Pibble knew what he was. He had the dragon look, bleak and subtle.

"You're Wilson," said Pibble. So Jenny had been right in her romancing.

"'Sright—while I'm in this hole, I'm Wilson. And you're Pibble."

"How do you do?"

"Not so good, but berrer'n you, cock. If it wasn't for the heart . . . Question is, if I sit in that chair, will I get out without my sending for someone to give me a heave? Not supposed to be in here, am I?"

"The other chair's easier. I usually . . . They slide."

"Well, if *you're* up to it, cock . . ."

Fully awake now, interested, almost excited—but still aware of the need to keep open the escape route into mumbling doze— Pibble elbowed himself a little up the pillows, watching his visitor all the time. Wilson slid the chairs about, seeming to take care to select an exact site for each of them. He nodded, bent and dusted the seat of the nearer chair with a large handkerchief which matched his pyjamas, a quirk proper to a man used to wearing expensive clothes in seedy places. Pibble was aware of his own mind registering the perception, but the awareness made him oddly nervous—as the ship's captain might be, glancing up at his wind-swelled sails, back at his level wake, all round at his poxed and dream-sodden crew now suddenly obedient and sailorly, and wondering how long it could last.

At last Wilson lowered himself into the chair. With the same heavy precision he took a roll of mints from his pocket, un-wrapped one and put it on the pad on his lip. He spoke without removing it.

"Like I say, just thought I'd take a look at you."

"For old time's sake," murmured Pibble.

The dragon-glance flickered, not surprised but acknowledging a level of mutual understanding.

"I don't remember as we ever run into each other."

"I don't think so, no."

Now, like a trap-door spider taking prey, the tongue flickered between the mauve lips and the peppermint was gone.

"Nearly, I dessay, once or twice. The Furlough bust-up, f'rinstance—wasn't you in on that?"

"On the fringe. A case that had some connections. Were you?"

"Was I? That'd be telling. Spent a year or two in Spain round about then—for my health, see?"

"Ah."

They contemplated each other for a while, openly, without side-glances. For Pibble, Wilson's presence was as it were totemic. It had power, power to exorcise the nightmare. He was too interested in this reality to indulge in senile and self-pitying imaginings. Now he became aware of something off-key about his visitor, something not wholly proper to the dragon-look. The look was there, certainly, but something, an element of emotionless malice, was not really functioning. The people of this type whom Pibble had known—not all of them criminals, but mostly—had been capable of doing things to other people which were literally incomprehensible. There was no way of imagining the springs of such malevolence; it was inhuman, but not bestial, either. Wilson had clearly had that capacity, most of his life, but now the gland had withered, the springs had dried up. It was as if the dragon had grown not kindly but at least sentimental in old age. Wilson's next remark, spoken as if already well into a train of thought, seemed to confirm this.

"You and me, f'rinstance, sitting here like this. One of us a rozzer all his life, and one of us summing else. It could so easy of been the other way round."

"I wouldn't have made a very effective . . ."

55

"I dunno about that. Plenty of nervy little fellers . . . Ever run into Sunny Macavoy?"

It was extraordinary how Wilson's company—the half-shared life, the common concerns—could revive shrivelled wits. An hour before, Macavoy's would have been at best a dream-name, its waking connotation irrecoverable.

"Con man? I never met him. Wasn't his line phony arms deals? Make anyone nervy, I'd have thought."

"Sure. He chose it. Did a bit of hotel thieving when things were quiet. Got nicked for that once. No, I'm a liar, twice. Last I heard there was some Palestinians looking for him what he'd got to put down the deposit on a load of plutonium, only it was just lead what he'd got some bent boffin to dope up so it would make a geiger-counter click. Might of been your cousin, some ways."

Wilson unwrapped another peppermint, his manicured but brutal fingers peeling the foil off whole, but then rolling it into a pellet and flicking it on to the floor. All his actions seemed completely considered, even to the deliberate discarding of a bit of waste. They were part of his style, of a life that had been an exercise of will, with the most trivial action performed in a way that emphasised the power to do it.

"Whatchew really in for?" he said suddenly.

"Why am I here? To live for a bit, I suppose. Then die."

"Nah. Come off it. You was never in Vice. You was never in the Porn Squad, uh? Nor Serious Crime, neither. Even if you *was* bent, which I don't remember hearing, it wasn't the sort of set-up that'd let you stack away enough to bring in six hundred nicker a week, pay for a bed in this place."

"Urr?"

"Besides, I hear as you come in from a grotty little lodging up in Hackney somewhere."

"Who told you that?"

"Little Miss Innocence what's always asking questions—she answers 'em too. Gives her a chance to talk about her pet detective."

"Jenny!"

"'Sright. I got interested when she mentions as you been a copper. Name like yours, it rings a bell, dunnit? First, acourse, I get it into my head as you're here to keep an eye on me—arter all, you must be ten years younger than what I am, so what are you doing in a place like this? Then she persuades me as you been reelly ill, and I start to get curious. Don't tell me you hadn't cottoned how much it was costing."

"As a matter of fact, no."

Pibble was unable to resent Wilson's questions. Fees were not a subject much discussed among the patients at Flycatchers, though other kinds of gossip were rife. There was, as it were, a tacit recognition that some people might actually find it hard to scrape the money together, might indeed be forced to leave for lack of funds, and thus effectively to die. Poverty to the inhabitants of Flycatchers was a terminal illness, and though minor ailments might be exchanged, like chat about weather, elsewhere there was a solid tabu. Wilson seemed unaware of this. There was a direct and dispassionate quality about him, an acceptance of the world as it is without whining or rancour—a fairly common trait among serious villains.

"So someone's finding the money," he said, "and it ain't the Police Benevolent Fund. Don't come you dunno who."

"I've got one rich friend. I hadn't realised how much it was costing him."

(Had refused to let my mind worry that bone, more like.)

"Ah, him. Saved his life once, dinchew?"

"So he chose to believe."

"Then why wasn't he giving you a bit of a hand before? Don't tell me—cause you hadn't let him know as you needed it. Stupid, that is. Cost him more in the end, dinnit?"

"I'm afraid so."

(Only I've still never asked for money. That matters. To him too.)

"All right," said Wilson. "I'll buy that. It's silly, but it adds up, like most other things. But there's summing as doesn't add up.

57

Here you are, no use to anyone no more, just waiting to die without causing no more fuss. Not my fancy, but I'll buy that too. What I won't buy is you getting up and getting dressed and going out and climbing that tower and finding George in the middle of the night. And don't give me that about hearing no shots, neither. Remember as I'm just a couple of rooms along and I know how the wind was that night. If a bloody howitzer had loosed off under your window you wouldn't of heard it."

Yes, Wilson would have made a good policeman. His voice had weight, emphasis which came from his refusal to emphasise any particular word. He gave no sign that the question interested him more than the others. If he'd been a policeman he'd probably have been bent, but he'd still have been more effective than a lot of the straight ones.

"Why do you want to know?" said Pibble.

"I'm curious."

"That doesn't . . . unless you think that whoever shot Tosca might, er, have been looking for you."

This time the pale eyes didn't flicker, but still somehow acknowledged the guess. It was as though their impassivity, till now habitual and unconscious, had become deliberate.

"Shouldn't of made his rounds that regular," said Wilson.

"He didn't that . . ." said Pibble, and cut himself off too late.

"Couldn't of, not that night, could he? Dead by then. But before that you could of set your watch by the time he went in and out under here. Stupid. Don't tell me as you hadn't noticed."

"I suppose I had. They run this place on a pretty tight routine, though . . ."

"Course they do, but George didn't have to pay no attention to that, did he? Trouble with him, he thought he knew it all. Look, when he was training, they must of told him not to do things all regular. That's right, innit?"

The question was not rhetorical, but spoken as though Pibble should know the answer. Wilson, leaning across to interfere with one corner of Pibble's jigsaw, had nudged a loose piece with his cuff and now, with the slightly altered angle, what had so far been abstract smudges and blurs became plainly representational—a bit of blue uniform with a belt across it. Of course. Tosca had been a policeman. Yes, the licences for the guns, for one thing, and Mike's attitude to that. Mike being here at all. A Chief Super.

"So what was you up to that night?" said Wilson. "You still haven't told me."

"I don't know myself," snapped Pibble, irritated by the interruption to his thoughts. Tomorrow, in an hour's time, even, these sharp-edged and potentially interlocking perceptions might have reverted to the usual slithering fuzz.

"You don't know," said Wilson impassively.

"I probably didn't know at the time, and I certainly don't now. All I can tell you is that a bit after Jenny left me I started to get up and dress, and while I was doing that I began to tell myself that I was doing it because of something I'd heard, in spite of the wind. I thought it was a shot. Even then I didn't know if it was true, and I certainly don't now."

"Hunch."

"I don't believe in hunches. I never did. They always let you down."

"Right. Remember Ferdy Greer?"

"I don't think so."

"After your time, perhaps. Hit man for the Blue Bear crowd. Drugged a bit. Mary Lou Isaacs told me this—she and me was quite good pals, once. Forget it. Ferdy. It was after some job, the pay-out. Everything gone like clockwork. Some very hard boys in the Blue Bear lot, so Mary Lou liked to have Ferdy around case one of 'em tried something. But that night there hadn't been no arguments and they was all sitting around having a drink and relaxing when Ferdy jumps up and says 'I'm getting out of this.' Summing in the way he says it, so Mary Lou looks at him, and he's dead white, and all he'll say is summing bad's coming, summing reelly bad. Born in a gipsy van, Ferdy, so Mary Lou shrugs and gives him a stack of tenners, and that's the last she sees of him.

Couple of hours later he's out at the airport with his passport and a ticket, getting on to a plane for Jamaica. Now, there's a rozzer in plain clothes on the gangway, looking for someone else, not Ferdy at all. Ferdy sees him and knows him but he walks past and is going up the gangway when the rozzer does a double-take and calls out to him to come back. It'd only have been a couple of minutes' chat, see—he couldn't of stopped him, and he wasn't wanted, nothing like that. But Ferdy's that nervous he's got his gun out—this was before the big hijacks had started, see—and the copper's dead almost before Ferdy's finished turning round."

"Yes, I remember. He tried to take the plane, didn't he, but made a mess of it?"

"'Sright. Funny thing about Ferdy—he was shyer with women than anyone I ever heard of. Kept a deaf and dumb girl, not much younger than what he was, but he treated her more like she was his daughter and he was shy even with her. That's how Mary Lou managed him, see, but even there it had its disadvantages. Mean as a ferret with men, Ferdy; didn't mind what he did to them— knock 'em off quick or watch 'em linger, it's all one. But suppose Mary Lou needed a woman roughed up or scared, she had to hire a different bloke. Well, there was this air hostess top of the gangway and spite of what she seen Ferdy do she gets out a smile for him—it's the training, I suppose. Automatic, doesn't mean nothing, but it hits Ferdy like it was a bit of lead pipe and he stands there, all goofy. Can't of lasted more'n a second but the girl spots what's up—you know how quick some of these tarts are, that sort of thing—and spite of he's got his gun on her she somehow knows he's not going to use it and she gives him a shove and gets the door shut and the plane taxis away with Ferdy still on the steps, no hostages, no plane, nothing. And he's shot a copper for no reason at all, 'cept that he had this hunch that summing bad was coming. He puts his gun in his mouth and knocks hisself off."

The interruption to Pibble's tenuously maintained reasoning processes turned out to have been no such thing. He half-listened as Wilson told the story—dull voice almost a whisper, small eyes studying glistening fingernails—but at the same time he was becoming aware of how hard it is for a certain type of man to take his secrets to the grave. Some do, almost gleefully, the miser's dead hands still clutching his bag of ducats; but others who have amassed their dangerous knowledge with the same ferocity discover in old age that their lust is for their secrets to live on, where breath most breathes, even in the mouths of men. Like a millionaire pouring out his money on some charity that will perpetuate his name, they spill the beans. The Wilson Foundation. No wonder a Chief Super had come down; he'd been on the case long before Tosca died, because Wilson was also a Super. A supergrass. Because of his heart they'd put him into a top-class nursing-home, and because of his importance they'd chosen one that was already a fortress, and on top of that they'd given him a bodyguard. With Wilson around, there couldn't be room for much else in their minds than the idea that Tosca had been killed in order to clear the way towards him. If that was true, the killers had made a mess of it, but at least it meant that the opposition was not squeamish.

"Is Mary Lou looking for you?" asked Pibble.

The cold eyes flicked towards him, then back to the fingernails.

"Fellers with rotten hearts," said Wilson. "You hadn't ought to go saying that sort of thing to them. Besides, she's in Switzerland, last I heard, having her innards taken out . . . Meet her ever?"

"Not to talk to. I saw her years ago. She was a defence witness in two of the cases when we broke the Smith Machine. I don't remember that she struck me as anything extraordinary."

"You wouldn't say that now, not if you saw her. 'Sides, there must have been summing, you remembering her all that long."

"Not really. It was my first big case, though . . ."

"Got you. The Smith Machine. There was a bent copper working for 'em, and a big 'un. Now, what was his name?"

"Richard Foyle."

"Right. A knight in shining armour with dirty underpants, that's him. And you was the young copper who opened it all up.

61

And Mary Lou . . . Now I heard summing about her in that case. What was it? I hadn't nothing to do with the Smith Machine myself, but somebody told me long after, when we was talking about Mary Lou . . . Got it. She wanted the Smith brothers sent down, spite of being a witness on their side, and she did her best to see that's what happened. Right?"

Pibble closed his eyes and tried to dredge the image out of the quicksands. *A pale child, dark, petite, nervous, biting her knuckles before she answered; starting well, then a faint hesitation and a recovery. A rather ordinary sort of girl—older than she looked, one came to realise—but a good choice by the defence for an alibi witness, ordinary and credible. Pouncer Malahide rising to cross-examine. The witness suddenly more nervous. The first self-contradiction. Pouncer doing his stuff. Witness going to bits, defiant and pathetic. Stir in court, a shared shiver of triumph along police spines—the alibi wouldn't wash after all. The Smiths were going down.*

"I wonder if you're right," said Pibble. "It certainly didn't strike me at the time."

"It wouldn't, not with Mary Lou. Remember what happened to the Smiths?"

"They got into a fight in Parkhurst. One of them died."

"And the other just didn't—got his skull bashed in, though, and his brain went sort of soggy. Spent the rest of his life in a home, and not so cushy as this place, neither. I sometimes wonder if Mary Lou didn't lay that fight on, somehow. She wouldn't fancy the Smiths coming out, trying to pick up where they left off, would she?"

"I don't know."

It was, of course, possible. On the other hand even apparently dispassionate historians like Wilson could become ensnared by the glamour of power, the common belief among criminals that everything that happens has been arranged for the advantage of one of the moguls of violence.

"How long ago was all that?" said Wilson. "Twenny-five years?"

"Thirty-one."

"Much as that? Water under the bridge, uh?"

If it was, then there must be some kind of eddy in time, set up by the bridge itself, for whenever Pibble stared over the coping he saw Foyle's face trapped there, turning and turning. He watched another peppermint flicker and vanish from the pad on Wilson's lip, and seized on it as the chance to turn the talk away from Foyle and the Smiths.

"Did you find it difficult to give up?" he asked.

"I've not bloody given up. Just laying off—part of the contract, see? But soon as this job's done with I'm taking my cash and flying out to Bermuda or someplace, where I can sit on the beach all day with a fresh box of Havanas beside my chair and watch the bathing girls do-dahing along the sand. P'raps the cigars will kill me, p'raps they won't, but one thing—I'm not going to die of sucking bloody Polos."

Pibble made a sympathetic mumble, and Wilson leaned forward, apparently roused for the first time.

"What else is there, my age?" he asked. "Girls? No thanks, except to look at. Never been much of a drinker, neither. But a good cigar, now . . . I shall miss George, for that."

"Uh?"

"My chauffeur, see? Took me out for a bit of a drive, fine days, where I could have a smoke in the back of the Jag without Miss Innocence or someone coming along and sniffing what I been up to."

"I see . . . What did you make of Tosca?"

Wilson leaned back in his chair and considered.

"Kind of life I've lived," he said, "you see a lot of rubbish. You don't run into a lot of fellers what you respect, if you follow me. You get used to rubbing shoulders with all kinds of scum, and it doesn't bother you. You take what you want of them, and you leave the rest. So you won't tell me I'm contradicting myself when I say I quite liked young George, but I knew he was rubbish. He needn't of been but he was, and I'll tell you for why. Because he fancied George Tosca so much. F'rinstance, he'd read a lot of books—always on about his reading—but he'd hardly thought about anything, 'cepting as it affected George Tosca. Vanity made him stupid, spite of him having his share of brains and more. Listen, you remember we was talking about how it might of turned out you being a villain and me being a rozzer?"

"Uh."

"I give you a caper with a bit of class, didn't I? Sunny Macavoy—he's got class, all right. But if George had been a villain he'd have been a ponce and nothing more. Yes, and not one of the gentle ones, neither. He had it in for women—you know the sort. Told me once he'd made a list of all the girls here and was crossing them off as he laid them. I dessay that's what he was up to in that room of his in the tower."

The wing of the nightmare brushed at Pibble's consciousness. He pushed it away.

"Was Tosca bent?" he asked.

"Depends what you mean. Bent enough to slip a box of Havanas into the glove pocket before we went out driving, and take a tenner off me for the service—that what you mean?"

"It's a start."

"He'd have bent more, and you wouldn't have had to wait long for it, neither. You must of met 'em, the fellers what gets a satisfaction out of doing wrong and telling themselves it's all right because it's them that's doing it."

Wilson knew his world, Pibble thought. There had been a touch of that sort of megalomania in Richard Foyle.

"You want to make anything of it?" said Wilson. "Wasn't a lot of opportunity for his going bent down here, was there?"

"I don't know. I've been wondering. If he wasn't stupid . . . If he knew the threat to you was serious . . . I mean, bodyguards get killed as often as the people they're supposed to be guarding . . . so you'd expect him to take his job seriously, if only because of the danger to himself. But he didn't. Made himself snug in the tower, never varied his rounds . . . Suppose he had been in touch with someone—they'd pay for news of your whereabouts, wouldn't they—then he might believe that he wasn't in any danger . . ."

"It's a thought," said Wilson, calm as ever. "Yes, it's a thought. You mention this to Mr Crewe?"

"No."

"I think you better."

"But . . ."

"Come better from you, see? I don't want him thinking . . . Not that there's all that to be scared of, now. If it was Mary Lou had George knocked off, she done a dumb thing. Before that, the rozzers had to keep their heads down, pretend they wasn't no such thing. Now with a murder to investigate Mr Crewe can put as many as he wants in here and no one's going to pass remarks. Still and all, I'd be glad if you told him what you just said."

"All right. Including your cigars?"

"Leave that out, cock, will you?"

"All right . . . These drives Tosca took you on, I suppose they were appointments to meet Chief Superintendent Crewe?"

"'Sright. Better'n taking the risk of his getting followed down here, see. You got your wits about you, anchew?"

"It comes and goes."

"Don't give me that. Miss Innocence, she says it's only your legs letting you down."

"Ur."

"And that's why I'm still not buying that crap about you hearing a shot. You knew what you was doing all right, dinchew?"

"Ur."

Pibble was already sliding down the pillow, as if by shrinking under the bedclothes he could withdraw his whole self into the safe shell of illness. But Wilson's presence, which had brought him out of that shell with the bait of interest and amusement, now compelled him with sheer power.

The chilly eyes watched him, unblinking.

"What I been thinking is this," said Wilson. "They found me somehow. Mind you, we been pretty careful, but now you given

65

me an idea how it might of been. They sent a feller out either to look the place over, or to see if he can't get a shot at me. I don't know what happened next. Could of been anything. Some of these young fellers these days, they get themselves so hopped up before a job they don't know what they're doing half the time, so George could of got knocked off almost by accident. Or the bloke might of thought he'd get a sight of me from the tower, and George caught him there . . . Even if I dunno exactly what happened, it makes a kind of sense. George in his seduction scene kit, waiting for that night's bit of skirt to come tiptoeing in, all shy . . . And what does he get? A hit man from Mary Lou. Yes, I can see it. What I still can't see is where you come in. You follow me? If I know what's going on, even when it's bad for me, then I can deal with it. But where there's summing as doesn't fit into the picture, then p'raps that means I got the picture all wrong. I don't like it."

At last Pibble managed to withdraw his gaze from the pale eyes. He closed them with a sigh and lay still. Blurrily a scene began to form in his mind but refused to coalesce. A collage of heroines with Lilian Gish faces crowded the tower stairs, swooned at what they saw on the leads, bent to remove some clue which would in fact have proved their innocence, and flickered wide-eyed into the storm . . .

"Lessee if I can get out of this chair," said Wilson.

Pibble opened his eyes and watched him rise. The body seemed to make no hideous effort, but a shadow of doubt—possibly even pain—twitched across the clay-coloured features. Wilson stood for a few seconds, withdrawn and silent, then nodded and shuffled towards the bed. Pibble stared up at him.

"Now see here, cock," said Wilson. "It ain't no use you lying there playing gaga. I'm not leaving you alone till you tell me what reelly happened. You never heard no shot, for a start. That's right, innit?"

"Ur."

"So what was you doing, climbing the tower?"

"Nothing to do with you."

"Reelly? Nothing to do with me? Or George Tosca? Or Mary Lou Isaacs?"

"No."

"You won't tell me no more?"

"No."

Wilson stood for a while, his hand teasing thoughtfully at his distorted lip. Pibble could feel the moral energy fading, and the weariness of old age becoming a different kind of bond between them. Suddenly Wilson gave a joyless little smile.

"You was always a straight copper, they tell me," he said. "Well now I'm going to bend you. We're going to do a deal. Your end is you forget to tell Mr Crewe about me having a few cigars on the side. My end is I don't mention as you been lying about them shots. Right?"

"Ur."

"So long. Stay bent then, cock."

Four

INCOHERENCE WOULD NOT quite come. The world was a desert, lit by an exhausted sun, but no monsters stalked there. The rocks were eroded into no particular shape, and the uninteresting scrub put forth a few drab leaves. Any liveliness of thought flickered like a lizard and was gone. Still, it was a daylight world, and the things in it stayed the same shape they always had been. Wilson was a villain helping the police. The body on the tower had belonged to a half-bent copper with a stamp-collector's attitude to women. And Jenny's lips had been icy—she had come straight to Pibble from outside, and had bedded down old Turnbull out of roster, because he wouldn't notice.

Unable to perform the mindswap into the preferable horrors of delirium, Pibble refused to contemplate these dreary truths. Instead, like the doomed prospector trudging across that desert, he kept his head bent and watched the movement of his own feet. Repetition. Habit. Habit. Repetition. Comfort. Tedium. In a poky little room a man could impose his own repetitions on his context. By putting his shoes in a precise place by the broken chair, by learning to wedge the self-opening door of the wardrobe until he does it without knowing he has done it, he proves his control of his kingdom. He can control time too, by never eating the snack that passes for supper until he has read at least two pages of yesterday's *Guardian* (filched from the dustbin where the neighbour with the artificial leg puts it—also by habit—each

68

morning). But in sickrooms, as in prison cells, these kingdoms are invaded. Unwilled repetitions are imposed by the machinery of the place, and by diminishing the man's control they whittle his life away.

There had been a prison cell once—at Pentonville, was it?—police seldom see men in their cells, but there'd been a strangling in the cell next door. A short, white tunnel, grey square of window, two beds, one hard chair, soil-bucket, locker, one picture—ship in full sail— taped to wall. No blankets on second bed. Prisoner—small, soft-spoken, earnest, unalarmed—had noticed nothing. Curious sense, emanating somehow from sailing picture, but filling whole room, of pure order, imposed by the prisoner himself. As if the picture had been placed there after a long process of measurement and decision, and could now never fit anywhere else. Conversation with warder outside cell door; "That's not much help. Pity there's only one of him. I thought you were overcrowded." "Can't put anyone in with him, sir. He drives them all mad. He's so bloody happy."

A discomfort which habit has learnt to cope with can be more comfortable than a habit imposed from outside. Threadbare blankets folded double seem somehow to give a more living warmth to an old body that has taught itself to huddle into half a bed than fluffy bedclothes smoothed and tucked in, with hospital corners, at the exact minute when the hospital schedule demands that the bed should be re-made. To know this, to be self-aware as Pibble usually was, does not prevent one from snarling at the innocent who makes the bed. And where love intervenes, or tries to, a tetchy jealousy crawls out to greet it.

Mrs Finsky came round with the lunch trays. Pibble managed to divert his lust to hurt her into a smile, sweet and feeble, and a claim not to be hungry. She stared at him for a moment with her glittering black eyes, then with an if-that's-how-you-want-it shrug took the tray away. Hungry at once, he lay and stared at the ceiling. Saliva spurted, and he had to swallow energetically to avoid dribbling. The sense of having been cheated, cheated by no one but himself, filled his universe. Nothing else mattered. There was nothing he could do about it. Now, like an ambush, the longed-for incoherence gripped him. He was starving, had been left to starve in the horrible room in Hackney, left to die . . . He was aware of tears streaming down his cheeks, and furious with himself for weeping so, he was on parade at Hendon with his legs quite bare and his face streaming with tears . . .

"Are you all right, Mr Pibble?"

"Ur?"

"Look, I've brought your lunch. Jenny said . . ."

He managed to shake the dream away and open his eyes. Maisie was standing by the bed, her soft cow-eyes looking amazed with trouble.

"Just a bad dream," he managed to mumble.

"Mrs Finsky said . . . but Jenny said . . ."

"All right."

"Do you want me to . . . she said . . . she didn't want to go . . . her mother . . ."

Clearer now, back in the real desert, Pibble blinked at these shreds of meaning. Maisie was Doctor Follick's personal nurse, but stood in for some of the other nurses on their days off. She and Jenny had adjoining rooms in the staff quarters, slightly cut off from the other nurses by being on the other side of the stairs. Jenny was fond of her, and grew angrily protective if you suggested that there was anything odd about her mental make-up. *"Look, she passed her exams, and you can't do that if you're thick. And she's good at her job, too—the Follicle wouldn't put up with her if she wasn't. She's all right, I tell you!"* But even Jenny couldn't have denied the oddness of Maisie's physical appearance. Though not the most beautiful of the Flycatchers bevy, she was almost ludicrously the most striking; tallish, thin to emaciation, stretched neck bearing a tiny, pale, small-featured face framed in a dahlia-like flurry of bright orange hair.

"I can manage, thanks," he said.

That seemed to be the right answer, confirming the rest of the interpretation: Tuesday, Jenny's day off, which she spent with her

70

mother. She had told Maisie to see that Pibble ate, and spoonfeed him if necessary, but then Mrs Finsky had said he didn't want his lunch . . .

"We've all got to do what Jenny tells us," he added.

"Yes! Oh, yes!"

She put the tray down and bent to help him up the pillows. Her mantis-like arms were extraordinarily strong.

"Jenny says I've got to . . ."

". . . stop and see that I eat it. If you like. And I'll probably need a wipe-up afterwards—the messy slops they give invalids. How's Lord Hawkside?"

"He's all right. I *think*. He's always gentle and kind with Marianne, but there's that woman he says is his sister, the Comtesse de la Folie. She *can't* be—I mean she's French and he's English—so I can't help feeling he's lying about her. But if he's a liar . . ."

Maisie had spoken with a sudden rush of energy, as though the adventures of these shadowy puppets were all she really wanted to talk about, all in a sense that was real to her. Presumably the scheming Comtesse would turn out to be only Lord Hawkside's step-sister, the result of a foreign entanglement on the part of his father, who had later enjoined him to help and protect the unworthy creature. There had been a lot of coaching-lore in the book so far, so possibly the Comtesse was going to die in a coaching accident; her one virtue seemed to be her vigour with the whip; no hint, of course, that she might use it on anything but horses. Ah yes, the cliff road—she'd go over there, in a wild midnight dash to escape the consequences of her plots . . . Pibble had once made the mistake of telling Maisie what was going to happen in her current book, and had thus ruined the reality of it for her. Jenny had been quite angry. So now he kept his guesses to himself, and only discussed the current state of play in the surprisingly intricate stories.

"If you can lie about one thing you can lie about anything, can't you?" said Maisie.

71

"You might think you had a really good reason."

"Oh, I do hope so. I like Lord Hawkside. I wonder why he won't let Marianne come to Wildfire Hall."

(Because he doesn't own it any more. *That* was what he lost in the wager with Sir Napier Fence, that false friend, who is of course hand in glove with the Comtesse, who—yes, *she* was blackmailed by Sir Napier into nobbling Lord Hawkside's horses before the coach-race, because Lord Napier knows that she's not even Lord Hawkside's sister. Had there been any hints of this? If so, Maisie hadn't included them in her re-tellings. Now, why was Sir Napier going to all this trouble, and making a play for Marianne as well, despite her obvious poverty? Because . . . because when Lord Hawkside married . . . No, when Marianne married, then Mr Jethro would produce the secret papers referred to in old Lord Hawkside's will, which proved that *she* was the true . . .)

"What's the story called, Maisie? I've forgotten."

"*The Owner of Wildfire.*"

"Ah."

"Shall I tell you what's happened so far?"

"Please."

For the moment the desert was not so dreary. There was a mirage. Bath, and Pall Mall, and the brooding mansion on the moors, all wavered into faint being. It was more amusing to watch them, despite their unreality, than to peer through their image at the true bleakness beyond. Pibble listened with care, and was gratified when Marianne met and recognised Old Frost, Lord Hawkside's former groom, sacked for theft and now begging in the streets. He would know about how the wager had been rigged.

"I'm sure Old Frost never stole anything," said Maisie.

"I expect the Comtesse framed him," said Pibble.

"Oh, do you think so? Why? She's got to have a reason."

That was the point. That was what gave the mirage its apparent solidity and at the same time proclaimed its unreality. Everybody had reasons for everything they did. Even Lord Hawkside's puzzling fits of moodiness would be explained in the end as

72

coming from purely practical causes, which could be put right by an adjustment of the machine. When it was all worked out, the plot would have the rightness of a solved crossword, and about as much meaning.

"Do you tell Doctor Follick all this?" he asked.

"I used to. Then I stopped."

Made fun of her, no doubt. Or did he? What did Toby, with his passion for clinical gadgetry, make of his unclinical, non-robotic nurse? On Pibble's visits to the surgery he had made no attempt to work her into his act, which he could easily have done—the conjurer's assistant, beautiful but dumb. In fact down there Maisie seemed like a different person, unobtrusive, competent, almost brisk. "Of course she adores him," Jenny had once said. "He likes being adored. If he had a dog it would be a red setter, a real sop-hound. She's a bit like one, isn't she? I'm a terrier—yap, yap." They had gone on to consider the doggy equivalents of the other nurses, and Pibble hadn't registered till now how perceptive she'd been about Maisie. There was nothing to prevent Maisie being a good nurse, just as red setters—all flop and sentiment at home—are presumably competent gun-dogs.

His interruption seemed to have blocked the flow of the story. He watched her drifting round the room, pushing the chairs about, apparently quite absent-mindedly, but in fact returning them to their normal positions, then counting out his pills from the drug locker concealed behind the wall-mirror—a typical Flycatchers arrangement, meant to hide even from the sick the paraphernalia of their sickness and the obscenities of age. If Tosca had really made a list . . . Yes, she would be near the top of it. Not as beautiful as Debora or Pauline, not as pretty, even, as Jenny, but somehow closer than any of them to the fantasies of lust. How old—how past-it—did you have to be to consider such a question quite objectively? Perhaps the time never came. Pity . . .

Tiredness swept over him once more. He pushed the tray away and let himself slide a little down the pillows. Maisie, who had been looking out at the cedar apparently lost in a dream of

Regency intrigue, noticed the movement at once, brought him his pills and the tumbler of water, helped him to cope without choking or slobbering, and eased him down to the horizontal. She picked up the tray with the same decisiveness, but then just stood there looking down at him. He was already floating off towards the nonsense-world of dream, but she remained part of the scenery, changed, though, to belong to the altering context. He felt the sudden shock of dream-alarm that precedes and signals the nightmare. Her eyes weren't human at all. Her hair flamed round the white passionless face. She took a seemingly endless breath.

"I was helping Jenny wash her hair," she whispered. "That's what I was doing. Helping Jenny wash her hair."

Five

HE SLEPT AFTER lunch. On "good" days, of which this was apparently one, he lay for a little more than half an hour in a dreamless dark, from which he usually half-surfaced into a comfortable in-and-out doze, full of a tangle of thought and memory and dream. When Jenny spent her rest-period with him this would prolong itself into rambling talk, often till tea time.

Today he woke almost fully, knowing that he had slept longer and deeper than usual and that Jenny wasn't there. Of course, it was her day off. But what . . .? There was something else. Shock. Just before he had gone to sleep he had . . . That's why he had slept like that—shock, not tiredness. He wasn't really tired. It was a "good" day, and he'd been thinking effectively. None of that now. Rest time. He ought to be dozing in and out of dream . . .

He let his mind begin to jumble through ancient detritus, but kept finding among the dusty relics something new and strange, connected with Jenny, or Mike Crewe, or the body on the tower. One part of him yearned to assemble these new pieces into a collection, to compare shapes, fit them together into whatever whole or wholes they ought to compose; this longing was over-ruled by a reluctance which disguised itself as tedium, though it was deeper than that. Occasionally, as if by accident, two or three fragments would coalesce into a shape which was almost . . . but then his mind would shy away, pick up an ancient toy worn beyond any recognition of origin, and play violently with that until the alarm and menace of that *almost* died away again.

The process was thoroughly unpleasant, and could not last. Soon he would be forced awake by the pressure of worry and then he would have to start to think. Unless . . . Deliberately he tried to will back the desolation which had engulfed him when Mrs Finsky had taken his lunch away. At least there was no thinking in that morass. But it wouldn't come. After all, this was a "good" day. A desert.

Suddenly, the desert was inhabited, not by a stranger seen trekking towards him out of the distance, enabling him to prepare a mask and a reason, but by an ambush. A voice at the door, a rattle of metal on timber. Lady Treadgold. Crippen.

Residents at Flycatchers did not often visit each other in their rooms. This was not a rule, but a code of manners. It was in the TV lounge and the bridge room and the morning room and the dining hall and the bar that encounters took place, alliances were formed, feuds fought. One went down there prepared for meetings, wearing the armour of almost-health. It was not good manners to play other roles than the stoic. But in one's own room one unbuckled, and was as feeble, ill, old as one chose. Naturally, one did not care to be seen in such a state, with the door of the mausoleum ajar and the odours of death seeping into the air.

Of course Lady Treadgold knew this, so came rattling into the room already talking. Her head was cocked sideways and a little forward, just the gesture she used when she rebid her own feeble suit knowing that her partner had every right to play the hand.

". . . so they were all against me," she said, banging her walking-frame forward for emphasis and hobbling after it. "I told them if only Mr Pibble was here he'd say I'd done the right thing. McQueen wouldn't have it. So in the end I had to come and ask you. You don't mind?"

"Come in. Would you like a chair? Shall I ring?"

"No, no, no, my dear man. I shall do quite well on my scaffolding. Now, listen. They were vulnerable, we were not. McQueen, on my right, dealt. I picked up one spade, eight hearts—eight, Mr Pibble, but only the Queen and tiddlers . . ."

Jabbering technicalities Lady Treadgold rotated herself and her frame until she presented only her monolithic rear to the bed. She manipulated the gadget at the side of the frame which unfolded a sort of canvas seat across it, so that it became what she called her "scaffolding", a support against which she could prop herself without the pain of sitting. Colonel McQueen had once told Pibble that she could sit perfectly well if she wanted to, but that she preferred to stand because it gave her a better view of her opponents' hands. Pibble, before his adventure, had sometimes spent the empty hours between tea and supper watching the regular game in the bridge room. He seldom played—the stakes were too high for him, the conventions too new and complex, his own attention span too short; but Lady Treadgold used the bystanders as part of her armoury, appealing to them to confirm the sanity of her crazier forays and taking their approval for granted before they had time to answer. Now he did his best to concentrate on her story, and as he did so became aware of an oddness about it.

"So there I was," she snapped, her stony blue eyes popping in the brick-red face. "Five hearts, doubled on my right. What would you have done?"

(Kicked the table over? Had a fit and fallen frothing to the floor? Challenged McQueen to fisticuffs?)

"Bid six hearts?" guessed Pibble, who had lost track half-way through.

She cackled as she settled on to her frame.

"Naughty, naughty. I won't say it didn't cross my mind. No, I redoubled."

"For a rescue?"

"My dear man! Nobody rescues *me*! They all passed."

"What happened?"

"Guess."

(Three down? Five? Seven? It had happened—but there was that oddness.)

77

"You made it."

"I did. I crashed the King and Ace of hearts, ran the rest of the trumps, threw McQueen in with his Ace of diamonds which he'd been too mean to get rid of, and forced him to lead into dummy's club tenace!"

(Yes. There it was. She'd come all this way not to appeal about something which had gone wrong, but to crow over something that had gone right. So she hadn't come for that at all.)

"Well done. I wish I'd been there to see you do it."

"I wish you'd been there to see McQueen's face, especially when I pointed out they had six diamonds cold."

"It's nice to know that life is going on without me."

"Life! You can't call it life, Mr Pibble. Not compared with what you've been up to. I want to know all about that. It's ridiculous, there must be at least a dozen policemen hanging around, looking as though they expected one of us to leap out of our wheel-chairs and shoot them, but they don't seem any further on, do they?"

"I'm afraid I really don't know much about it."

"But you found George's body, didn't you? Nurse says you'd spotted something was up and went out to check. I'd have done the same in your place—never could keep my nose out of mischief. Now don't tell me you haven't told them about George; that's not very public-spirited of you, Mr Pibble, though of course black-mailers deserve everything they get."

"I'm sorry, I . . ."

"Still, murders are murders."

"Yes, but . . ."

"Now don't interrupt. It tires you to talk, and it's never tired me. In any case I can see you aren't going to admit anything; this idiotic passion for secrecy. Not that I really disagree with it—life wouldn't be very interesting if there weren't any secrets to sniff out—but I spotted George was a blackmailer the minute I clapped eyes on him. He had blackmailer's ears. There was a young feller used to hang around the Cri in Monte—lounge lizards we called them then, of course—sucked poor Didi Towcester dry over a

78

diary he stole from her dressing-table. Didi was *not* particular who she shared her bed with, remember—oh, my dear man, forgive me if you were one of them—but Towcester had this idiotic faith in her. It sometimes strikes me that the aristocracy were deliberately breeding for stupidity, as though it was a good point, like a mastiff's jaw . . . yes, George had exactly the same shape of ears. He was a blackmailer all right."

"Who . . ."

"Oh, everybody. That rather attractive outsider who calls himself Wilson, for instance. I don't know whether you've noticed him—he never comes into the public rooms, if he can help it. He's a criminal too. I must admit, Mr Pibble, that I've always had a soft spot for criminals ever since that gang tunnelled their way into Trubshott's all those years ago. It still gives me the weeniest frisson of joy to think of all my old friends with their emeralds and bonds and guilty secrets tucked away in Horace Trubshott's vaults because they said to themselves Horace is such a *solid* man—a bore of bores is all they really meant. I've known girls who've gone to bed with Horace because it seemed the only way to stop him talking about his bank, and all the time anyone could burrow into it and sneak off with . . . Did you know that's where the Ilford rubies were? Typical of Freddie Ilford to get that far without understanding that once he'd collected the insurance the rubies were a millstone round his neck, because he had to hide them: far better to get them properly stolen in the first place . . . Ah, yes, I've no doubt George knew something about the soi-disant Mr Wilson, and I've no doubt he used it."

"George? Did he try . . .?"

"Of course he did. Why else do you think I'm telling you all this? He'd hardly been here a week before he offered to take me out for a drive in Wilson's car. I took him up, of course—no point in not amusing yourself, is there? I could see those weaselly little eyes glancing at me, thinking *I'll get the old girl between the sheets and she'll tell me what she didn't ought*—and I would, too. It's one of those mistakes you don't learn by. You tell yourself you'll have your fun and you'll give nothing for it, but you let them have everything they want in the end; it's because . . . When I had my looks it was *me* they wanted. The awful thing is you can't help trying to make it seem like that still, by giving them what they do want . . . Poor George Tosca. No, I shouldn't say that. I mean, it might sound disgusting, but he wouldn't have worried. That type, what they enjoy is power, and you can have as much power over an old bag like me as you can over a pretty young innocent. More. Don't worry, Mr Pibble, it never happened. I've given it all up, but George wasn't to know that. Now that I can't bend or wriggle—not much point in lying there like a log with a hole in it . . . Yes, Mr Pibble, he tried me . . ."

She fell suddenly silent, swaying a little on her frame. Her eyes, blue as bathroom tiles, stared at Pibble without seeing him. The pearls on her powder-pink twinset changed their hue with a steady rhythm as her deep breaths altered the impact of light on them. Her face was set like an image on a terracotta urn, weathered, enduring, pagan. To the best of Pibble's memory she had never spoken to him, or to anyone else in his hearing, about any other subjects than bridge or food. She was a terrible old woman, but he felt drawn to her, and only faintly jealous of the fires that still fumed through her half-eroded clay.

"Well, aren't you going to say anything?" she said angrily.

"Ur? Yes. If he was . . . Who else? Colonel McQueen . . ."

Anger became a snort of contemptuous laughter.

"Hopeless! My dear man, hopeless! You could no more blackmail poor Weeny than you could blackmail *you*! He's never done *anything*. Think of it—two and a half million to play with when he was twenty-one, and all he could do was join an *infantry* regiment! Mary Wookey decided to take him on—had to hypnotise him into proposing, I shouldn't wonder. She had an eye like a basilisk, little Mary; showed him one thing he could do, and let him do it for a few years. Result, eight daughters, all as plain as hake. Even Mary gave up then, told him to learn bridge, not that that got him totally off the other; poor Weeny, I've seen him go quite white with lechery watching that nurse of Follick's, the carrotty one with the extraordinary face, but of course being Weeny he won't have dared try . . ."

"I thought in the war . . ."

"Oh, yes, the war," said Lady Treadgold impatiently, as if referring to a village fete which she hadn't troubled to attend. "He got a DSO and some other medals, didn't he? Yugoslavia or somewhere. Nothing for George Tosca there—too young to realise that anything that happened in the war might still matter. Too stupid, too—cunning but stupid—just like a woman that way. Do you remember Nora Scarston-Smith, for instance . . ."

"I helped investigate her murder. She was Nora Bessmuller by then."

"My dear man! My dear man! I had no idea! How too delicious. You mean to say you sent my nephew Tommy to the gallows! How incredibly bizarre!"

"I was only one of a team, rather junior," said Pibble, but she hadn't heard him. She was laughing silently, swaying on her frame and flinging out pudgy, ringed hands to balance against each lurch. Her head was thrown back and her mouth was wide open so that he could see right in among the blackened teeth. Suddenly he perceived what she had been before she had become this other creature, some fifty years ago, a strident frivol, rich, pretty, hard as the Lalique mascot on the bonnet of her Bugatti tourer, laughing like that in a brownish snapshot of a Riviera picnic party. He remembered Bessmuller. *Striped trousers, black jacket, round face sweaty with strain, the man's accent thickening as he paced his many-mirrored drawing room and tried to explain to Dickie Foyle (impassive, sitting on the arm of a deep chair and swinging one leg gently to and fro) the shock of what he had found in the swimming-pool in his basement. Bessmuller, adviser to governments, millionaire of his own making—it had been the great man's naivety that had made a fairly commonplace piece of butchery belong in the fantasy world of pure horror. That he should have not grasped, even after a year of marriage, what kind of person his*

81

showpiece wife in fact was. That the world was run by men who knew so little about the world. Now Pibble could not have put a face to the young idiot they hanged; the scene in the swimming-pool was a blotchy vagueness of green and scarlet; but he could still have counted the sweat-beads along Bessmuller's upper lip and got the number right.

Lady Treadgold stopped laughing.

"Don't tell me you didn't know Tommy was my nephew," she croaked. "Well, why should you? He was only my step-nephew in any case . . . Funny, I came up here thinking I'd have to work round to what I wanted to ask you about, and not let you know that was really why I'd come, but now you've told me about Tommy . . ."

For once, she hesitated. Pibble understood the dilemma. In her curious world-view, his connection with her nephew's death was a recommendation; not a total guarantee of trustworthiness, but analogous to an introduction to a tradesman—a decorator, say or a couturier—who had done satisfactory work for a friend. But she didn't want to offend Pibble by saying so. He produced his sweet-old-man smile.

"Well," she said slowly. "George told me something, or half-told me. While all these policemen are here, they might as well do something useful. I want you to get them to look into Archie Gunter's death."

"Sir Archibald . . ."

A shadowy figure, wavering among the mistinesses of Pibble's diminished perceptions when he had first come to Flycatchers. Wizened but military, with a remarkable bray.

"Hasn't it struck you, Mr Pibble, that this is a very expensive way of dying? We don't all have shipping millionaires to pay for us."

Pibble managed not to blink. If she knew that, then there might be tatters of truth in the rest of the gaudy gossip she was laying out before him.

"Yes, of course, but . . ."

82

"Then who is it expensive for, my dear man? Not for me, not for Archie Gunter, not even for poor Weeny. It doesn't matter to us how much we spend, does it, provided the money doesn't run out before we do? It's our heirs, poor darlings, who suffer. Now I knew Archie well. He was a fathead, but I liked him. He wasn't a rich man—comfortable, but not by any means rolling—and those girls of his were as fond of him as anybody could be of a stuffed-shirt ambassador; not that I'm against the FO—does a very useful job, I say, getting all those clever-clever nincompoops out of the country and into embassies in places like Bolivia where they won't do any harm. Don't look at me like that, my dear man, I know what I'm talking about, what with poor old Treadgold being one of them until he had to retire after that business with the fertility dancers in Mali; all my fault, though as a matter of fact he was delighted to resign and take up breeding his bantams . . . bantams, Mali . . . never regretted a second of it, myself . . . and at least what I did was popular with the native section of the audience . . . ah, yes, they were fond of him, I suppose, but they *had* been looking forward to their nest-egg. Perfectly happy about his staying here for a few months and then quietly fading away—they were about ten thousand quid fond of him, at a guess—but when he started getting better . . . What's the name of that play now, the one about the feller with the daughters, he starts off potty and finishes totally bonkers? Shakespeare, isn't it? That's the worst of the diplomatic service, having to go and sit through Shakespeare in Portuguese and Tamil and so on—bad enough in English, but in Hungarian! Lear, that's the feller's name, I must have watched it a dozen times and I always sided with the daughters. Why, my own father—I'll tell you about him some other time . . . Ah, yes, I remember one of Archie's gels, the fat one, coming down here to take him away because he was better, and he dug his toes in. I saw her saying goodbye to him, and if ever a real woman could have played one of those Lear gels! You see what I'm driving at? Of course it was the other one who fixed things up, and there, five weeks later, poor Archie wasn't even an ex-ambassador any more . . ."

"There'd be a post mortem and inquest."

"No, not always. I don't know about post mortems, but we don't always have inquests. Was there one on Archie? I think there was. But you've got to remember people are dying here all the time, so they don't . . . You won't remember Bertie Foster-Banks, of course. He died three years ago. No, Mr Pibble, Bertie had never done anything in his life except gamble and play practical jokes on people, and he carried on like that after his stroke. He'd bet on anything, and since he couldn't get out to the casinos he started making a book on which of the patients here would be the next one to pop off. Rank bad taste, and some of them wouldn't touch it, but it gave the rest of us a bit of fun, trying to wheedle stable news out of the staff—you can imagine it, Mr Pibble—and Bertie upsetting the odds with his hairy great spiders he'd bought from that joke shop in Holborn; not very popular with the doctors, you can imagine, but Bertie was a shareholder so they couldn't have him slung out, and some of the stuff-pots complained, and the nurses all hated him. Isn't it interesting who they take against? I gather you're *quite* a favourite, for instance . . . but you see the trouble was, from Bertie's point of view, that the book kept going broke because too many favourites romped home; the people who were supposed to die, died . . . But I was thinking only last week that supposing Bertie'd been running his book these last two years he'd have cleaned up handsomely— we've had half a dozen outsiders popping off when they looked as if they might have years in them . . ."

"Yes, but . . ."

"It doesn't have to be one of the doctors; in fact I don't see how it could be. Difficult for the non-residents, and I know your friend Follick was in America when Archie died . . . of course, anybody could have wanted to do away with Bertie Foster-Banks. I can't think how the shareholders put up with him, but Archie was a dear . . . suppose the shareholders . . . no . . . let's assume it was one of the doctors, Mr Pibble."

"But what do they . . ."

"Get out of it? Money, Mr Pibble. Money. Quite a lot of it. Listen, some old buffer, as it might be you, starts to get a bit doddery and his family decide to put him into kennels; that's been going on for ages, but do you remember when that Socialist woman with the tiresome voice changed the rules, so that the Health Service couldn't pay half the cost any longer? That's when your next of kin started having delicate little conferences with your doctor . . . 'We're all very fond of dear Daddy, but how long do you think . . .' Very tricky on both sides, to get it going, just like those tacky little chats one used to have at the beginning of a seduction before it all became so easy, though it's funny how there were always some men . . . I remember a Belgian bishop in Florence, now, what was his name? The Hound of Heaven we called him, because he got you in the end—you'd start off in some Contessa's drawing room, eating little cress sandwiches and talking about Mussolini, and you'd find him staring at you as if you were a halibut he was thinking of buying and wondering how to cook, and you'd decide he was a gruesome little creep, but by the time you said goodbye he'd actually hypnotised you into going to look at his icon next morning, and you'd go, too, despite knowing just what you were in for, like a visit to the dentist . . . yes, somebody like that in your team and you'd soon have the dutiful daughters telling you exactly how fond they were of dear Daddy and getting out their cheque-books to prove it."

"But that'd be killing the goose . . ."

"Plenty more geese around, and the golden eggs weren't going to the doctors anyway. But suppose this daughter of yours goes and lays a nice little nest-egg in a bank in Switzerland, tax-free, too—now if you could get the mysterious Mr Wilson to talk he'd tell you all about the advantages of tax-free income."

"But which of the doctors . . ."

"*That's* what I'm telling you I want them to find out . . . but do you know, I've just had the most extraordinary idea about Mr Wilson. I wonder why I didn't think of it sooner. I know who he is!"

"Ur?"

"Just about when you came here. The papers were full of it, and then went dead. Now let me see—I was interested because of Horace Trubshott—there was an informer, and the police were keeping him somewhere, and he was going to tell them enough to put half the criminals in London in gaol . . . I wonder how I can find out if I'm right? . . . You won't—no, of course not . . . but there was that extraordinary woman Bunty Jaques got hold of; Bunty swore she was running her own gang. I could write to Bunty . . ."

"I don't think . . ."

"Why on earth not? It's a free country."

She stared at him, outwardly stony with affront, but just as obviously enjoying his dilemma.

"Sir Archibald's death," he murmured. "You want them to take you seriously. Supposing you're right about Wilson—I don't know . . . you see . . ."

She smiled with malicious triumph.

"I *am* right. I always know. I wish I could remember that woman's name—something Jewish, I'm sure . . ."

"Toffs, they make me mad!" Foyle used to say. "Anything they do, it's all right because it's them doing it." A newspaper photograph of some titled politico pouring champagne into the glass of a known villain, both men in grey toppers, Derby Day in full swing around them; another of a yacht-load of countesses, the very deck they lounged on paid for by heroin profits. "It gives the silly bitches a kick, going into the cage and stroking the tiger." Foyle—he had been a tiger too. Perhaps it was that that had enraged him.

Pibble sighed. It was far from impossible that one of Lady Treadgold's circle had made friends with Mary Lou Isaacs.

"Don't you see?" he said. "The police aren't likely to be very co-operative if you spoil their plans by broadcasting Mr Wilson's real name, supposing you're right about it."

She pouted, wanting it both ways.

"They should do their duty, whatever *I* do," she said.

86

"On the other hand, if I were to tell them about your guess—still only supposing it's right—it would incline them to take your views on Sir Archibald's death more seriously."

"You mean they think I'm a stupid old woman," she snapped. "Well, they're wrong."

She ignored Pibble's mumbles of protest by heaving herself from her frame, turning, and stumping towards the door. Once there she turned again and glared at him.

"They're wrong," she said, her face now redder than ever with effort or anger. "I have all my wits about me. I may be stupid about the things the clever-clevers are good at—books and plays and stuff like that—but I know about people. People are my hobby—no, that's not strong enough—they're my food, they're the air I breathe. I understand 'em, better than anyone you'll ever meet. All right. To show your friends I'm not stupid, you tell 'em what I say about Mr so-called Wilson. And to show *you* I'm not stupid, Mr Pibble, I'll tell you something else. When you marry Nurse Blayne I'll send you a wedding present."

Without waiting to see how the shaft struck she banged out through the door and was gone.

He closed his eyes and lay in a dull haze. The shaft had struck, but into a mind already half-anaesthetised by the effort of argument. He was aware that she had said something of importance, not the nonsense about Gunter's death; that in the clatter of gossip lay a distinct message, like a human signal in the mess of radio noise that spreads between the galaxies. Not long ago his tuning to such signals had been sensitive and precise, but now the knob that controlled it kept slipping, revolved uselessly. All he got was noise, but what noise! Huge energies split from a dying star. Grotesque.

Without any lurch his mind was back among the grotesques of childhood. Ted Fasting, all buttocks, bent over his prize onions; Miss Amelia Barton, with the whiskery wart on her upper lip, lurked in her doorway to kiss any small boy she could grab; Joe

Pritchett shuffled to the pub in his Sunday best, with yellow slippers on his feet. That was how children saw the world, filling it with neighbours and strangers who are cartoons of goodness, of absurdity, of danger. Later on, the cartoons came into drawing, lost their grotesqueness, were human: Ted Fasting's buttocks less obvious than his guessed frustrations, Melly Barton's wart hardly noticeable in the face that held her pleading eyes. But with age the grotesques return, joined now by a new comrade, the central figure, the observer who has been child and then adult and has registered the others all the time against a scale of normality which is himself, only to realise that after all he is as distorted as any of them, a tottering body inhabited by a wavering mind, absurd and obscene. Absurdity and obscenity creep along, and their trail slimes the past. Entrancing childhood was aimed at this end.

"Had a good day?"

"Yes, I think so."

"You sound a bit tired."

"Lot of visitors. Two. Felt like a lot."

"It isn't fair. Days when I'm here you go gaga, and days when I'm away you entertain the world with sparkling conversation."

"What did you do?"

"Rather a beastly morning. I had to hold Mum's hand while she gave her tenant notice. When Dad ran off she split the bungalow in two and let half of it. This bloke sounded all right, but he keeps trying to run her life for her. You know, the worst thing about it was how nice he was. He couldn't understand why she wanted him to go, and actually she hasn't any legal right to turn him out, but he was quite charming, and of course that made Mum feel miserable with guilt so in the afternoon I took her to a garden centre and she bought three clematises and two daphnes and what looked like a bramble and some other things that didn't look like anything except twigs stuck into pots. That's where I get it from, I suppose."

"Ur?"

"Vegetables," she said, enigmatically. She had been putting his clothes away as she spoke. She looked younger than ever in her tee-shirt and jeans, a school-child almost. In three years she would be thirty, but time appeared not to have noticed her, to wander past year after year without bringing her up to date. She wasn't supposed to be working tonight, or to come into the Residents' Wings out of uniform, but she had managed to make a regular exception for him. He watched her with pleasure, and was instantly aware of a slight change in mood as she turned from the wardrobe.

"That reminds me," she said. "I couldn't ask you yesterday. Your hat's vanished."

"Blew off, I'm afraid, my dear. Sorry. Only thing I can call my own, as the Lady said to Doctor Joh . . ."

She had taken three quick strides across the room and was staring down at him.

"You were going outside all along," she whispered.

"Ur?"

"You were going outside all along. You put your hat on. That story about waiting for George in the kitchen and him not coming . . ."

She gripped his hand with both of hers and pressed it, hard, as though trying to extrude the truth from him. He lay still, gazing up, as the fences of his carefully reconstructed Eden withered and the desert rolled in. In a second she would guess the truth.

"Coat," he murmured. "Put on coat. Put on hat. Don't think about it. Coat. Hat. See if you can find it, Jenny."

She shook her head slowly.

"Your friend Mike came yesterday. I told him you weren't up to seeing him. I think he really wanted to talk to you. He said you were one of the best detectives he'd ever met, in a certain sort of case. He said this was it . . . Jimmy, you knew all along, or guessed. You went to look."

"I want my hat. It's mine."

He had summoned this wish as a defence against her, but now it

89

was all he could think about. Without his own hat, his last worldly possession, he would cease to be Jimmy Pibble, become a zombie, animated only to wear the alien clothes in the cupboard, to be an object for Jenny to nurse, a fraction of the Flycatchers' income.

"Honestly!" she snapped, then laughed. "I'll try to find your stupid hat for you. When did it blow off?"

"Going along the colonnade."

"I thought you didn't remember any of that."

He said nothing. She nodded and turned herself, like a car passenger who can only read a map in the direction of travel. Wind over her right shoulder—she knew that—he could almost feel its rush; could she too?

"Out there," she said, pointing decisively. "Those bushes by the croquet lawn. If it's not there it'll have blown all the way to Godalming."

"If they haven't found it already," he said.

She swung back, head cocked on one side, half smiling and half frowning, improvising the charade.

"If they have . . . I suppose you can still tell them it's yours. That bit about your coat. You can make them believe that, can't you?"

"Ur."

"I think you're quite extraordinary! This sort of thing *and* Doctor Johnson. What did he say to the lady, anyway?"

"Madam, do you call my heart nothing?"

She bent as if to look at his hand, which she was still clasping in hers. She lifted it slightly, put it down and let it go, then looked at him.

"About his hat?"

"No, about her coffee-pot. But it's the wrong way round. You're supposed to be saying it to me."

"Do I have to call you madam?"

"Ur."

Waking again. He was the yokel at the fair, tricked every time by the illusion. Under which flowerpot lurks the stuffed mouse?

90

There, surely . . . No, only the emptiness of dream. But through several layers of non-waking rambled the same figure. As far as he knew he had never before dreamed about any of the inhabitants of Flycatchers—they belonged to their own non-world—but now, of all people, Colonel McQueen kept trying to break into the misty adventures, more nonsensical even than usual, and tell Pibble something that mattered. In one of the last layers before true waking the message at last came through. Pibble was sitting on a sunlit beach, on a hard upright chair. He was about forty. The sand and sea were quite empty. Then the dream surface quivered, and he and Mary, still on the beach, were playing bridge. It must be an immense tourney. The tables spread all along the sand. The cards in his hand had no cohesion. He made a plan, but when he started to play to it the necessary elements were no longer there. Colonel McQueen playing at a neighbouring table, flung down his hand and said, "The rest are mine." After that Pibble and McQueen were paddling in the thin froth of the wave-margins and McQueen was saying, "Of course it looked hopeless, but there was one distribution which could save me, so I played as if it was true. And it was."

At this point, still some time before dawn, Pibble woke. He lay for a while, registering the message at first and then discovering its total unimportance. He slept again, without apparent dreams, but his mind must have continued on its own erratic course, because when he woke to face the day it had made itself up. He would assume that Jenny had been out on the night of the murder, and had gone to the tower, but she had not been the latest on Tosca's target-list, and she had not killed him either. So far, so good—that was the assumption. Now he had to satisfy himself that it was true.

91

Six

PAIN—OR RATHER soreness. Pibble sat in the outer of the two offices which the police were using as an Incident Room, and waited. Outside the window, beyond a ridge of roof, a scurry of sharp-edged clouds moved north behind a bat-winged cedar. A uniformed constable had given up his chair to him, and was leaning against the wall by the door, and a plain-clothes sergeant sat at a desk, busy on the familiar task of reducing a mess of notes to typed coherence.

Dressing had not been easy—harder than on the night of the "adventure", in fact; the bruised muscles of his left leg had grumbled and almost mutinied; nor had they liked the cautious walk through the corridors. But he had not allowed himself to think about pain until it was over, and then he discovered that it had not really counted as pain at all. True pain, the proper shrilling fire, nowadays lived deeper in. Though the anguished nerves might be on the surface, something told him that its source lay near the marrow, or in the nooks around the diaphragm. Surface injuries no longer hurt with the old urgency. It was as though morale at the frontiers had half-collapsed; a few lackadaisical nerve-endings might tap out messages of insult by the outer world—Pibble could almost see them, slouched in their patched and windswept guard-posts and gazing in a weary stupor at the latest horde of wild bacteria to sweep yelling through the passes—but true pain no longer seemed like an invader. Any day now it would be applying for naturalisation papers.

The idea still frightened him. He had never experienced pro-longed pain of that order, but he had seen it. *A boy writhing in a doorway off the Portobello Road; Scottie Mason had helped Pibble drag him there while they waited for the ambulance, because his writhings threatened to smash the spindle-legged furniture in the shop. In the street-lights the boy's face was blue-purple; he scream-ed, and contorted into impossible attitudes; foam frothed his lips. Scottie and Pibble could not look at each other, nor at the boy; they were helpless, pierced by the screams and the pain, no notion what to do. Windows were slamming up, heads peering out . . . Somebody must have phoned the shop-keeper, who arrived after the ambulance had left, whispering, scholarly, unappalled. He had shown them the snake. His safe, you see, was almost as old as the furniture in the shop, so he had kept the snake in there. The boy, presumably, had put his hand in in the dark . . . Lansdowne Crescent next morning. Smart little front garden, magnolia stellata in full flower with flame-coloured tulips beneath it. Boy's father a chancery lawyer, doing well; mother attractive, down-to-earth; boy their only. Both stricken—but they hadn't had to stand like Pibble and Scottie by that doorway and listen to the boy dying . . .*

"'Lo, Jimmy. Glad tŏ see you up."

He glanced up and saw that Mike Crewe had come in from the outer door, and was standing there, actually looking pleased at the sight of him.

"Penny for your thoughts," said Mike.

"Scottie Mason."

"Villain?"

"No. On the beat with me—Notting Hill, before the war. Left to join up. Got killed, I think. Africa."

"Friend of yours, though?"

"Not really. Just the same station. Saw the same . . ."

Pibble let his voice trail off, but Crewe interpreted the horrors from it. He nodded.

"Some things you don't forget," he said. "Come in. Shall I give

93

you a hand?"

"No. I can manage if I take it slowly . . . There."

Mike held the door of the inner office and Pibble followed him in. The two rooms, unlike most Incident Rooms, were real offices, but already the police-flavour hung strong around them, the sense of being worked in at all hours, of boredom laced with strain, of papers not processed and filed as in an ordinary office, but endlessly re-read and re-combined in the hope that with each sifting a missed nugget might emerge. Cass was sitting at the desk, staring at the ceiling. He looked less pleased than Mike had to see Pibble.

"Got your man, then, Chief?" he said. "The least likely person, I notice. That's what I call artistic."

"It's part of his world-domination plan," said Mike. "Which chair'll suit you, Jimmy? No, stay where you are, Ted. Anything new?"

He tweaked an upright chair round and sat on it with its back-support jutting up between his thighs and his arms folded across the top. The light from the window fell half-sideways across his face, emphasising how the smooth, almost babyish contours Pibble remembered had been weathered by the gritty wind of the years.

"One bit," said Cass. "More on my side than on yours. Remember me saying that the kitchen staff had a little more to give? I've got it now. They were supposed to hang on till Tosca turned up to close the mortice lock behind them, but they didn't that night because the Irish lady's nephew was playing in a football match and it was on the telly, so when Tosca was late they just slid away and left the door on the Yale. He was supposed to be there at eight twenty, and they gave him ten minutes extra."

"How do you fit it in?" said Mike.

"Two points. From eight thirty anybody could have got out of the house."

"They'd have to know."

"Maybe. The other point is, why didn't Tosca show? Perhaps

94

he was dead already."

"Not if Jimmy heard the shot."

"Cedar banging off. Eight thirty's well inside the pathologist's limits."

"You can't have them both. If he was dead already, whoever did it couldn't have gone through the kitchen. The staff were still there." ·

"Then I'll take point two."

Mike nodded, outwardly accepting the argument as sound, but at the same time somehow boring—an angle he didn't want to think about. Pibble was aware of a tension between the two policemen, not originally of dislike, but of a disagreement that could eventually build into animosity. It wasn't easy for either of them, clearly, with their different ranks and loyalties and interests in the case.

"You got anything, Chief?" said Cass.

"Not me. Jimmy has, though."

"Ur!"

"I called on our friend on my way in—that's why I'm late. He says you've got an angle, Jimmy."

"Wilson?"

"That's the boy. I'm glad you've had a word with him. I'll be interested to know what you make of him."

"Big fish."

"He tells me you spotted who he was."

"What he was. I don't know his real name, but he good as told me the rest."

"He *does* like an audience. Yes, he's big—bigger than he realises—if we can use him. You remember how it goes; you get a quiet period with the usual bit of random bother in it, and perhaps you relax; then you get a period with the bother still random, but somehow on a bigger scale—that's where we are now, by my reckoning; and then all of a sudden, while you've been sitting on your backside, you find the villains have got themselves organised, a whole new generation have learnt the trade, they've sorted out

95

their pecking order, invented new sorts of villainy and new ways of pulling old jobs, and zap, they're on top. This time, if all goes right, they won't be on top and half of 'em will be inside."

"If you can use him?"

"Grasses! Batty Perrin, for instance. Came in with a list as long as your arm of the men who'd been working the lorry capers all over the North-West. The judges threw the whole lot out."

"Yes. I read about that. I remember Batty. I was surprised you . . ."

"Not me, mate. I put in a memo saying it wasn't worth the risk. Half of what Batty gave us were grudge cases, and he was too thick to see what would hold . . . But Wilson's different, don't you think?"

"Yes, but even so . . ."

Crewe sat for a moment, chewing the knuckle of his thumb.

"Of course it's all very iffy . . . D'you think he'll scare, Jimmy? He can't back out, you see. We've got enough to put him down for fifteen years, and he doesn't want to die in gaol. But suppose he scared. He might try Batty's line, mixing enough duff gen in to get the whole lot thrown out. Oh, he'd be in trouble, but he might *think* he'd get away with it, telling us he'd kept his side of the deal, and the villains that he had done them a favour. So it matters whether he'd scare."

"You mean they couldn't get at Wilson, so they killed Tosca to scare him?"

"It's one theory. I can't say I care for it much—for one thing they'd need to know that Tosca was that easy to get at."

"He doesn't seem to have taken his job very seriously."

"He was top of his course for pistol shooting," said Crewe, ticking the points off on his fingers. "Ditto for unarmed combat. Ditto for emergency driving. Second for swimming. Straight As for the paperwork. IQ a hundred and thirty-something. Teetotaller . . . Just the man for the job, apart from being a rank bad policeman. Wilson says you've got an idea about him."

"It's hardly even that, but . . . suppose your theory's right,

96

you've still got to explain how the villains knew Wilson was here. Also why Tosca was taking his job so casually. He wasn't stupid. He must have worked out that the bodyguard is in just as much danger as the target."

"*He* told them, you mean?" said Mike. "Yes . . . What do you think, Ted?"

"I quite like it," said Cass, stretching like a waking cat, and making the movement into a gesture of interest, almost an apology for earlier boredom. "I was on one of those courses myself, when I was a sergeant. They laid quite a bit of stress on variation of routine. One way or another he seems to have decided he wasn't in any danger, so he could afford to take it easy and go James-Bonding among the staff here. He seems to have laid half the nurses, Mr Pibble, and had his sights on the other half."

"But if you accept that," said Mike, "you've let the Blue Bear lads into the picture . . ."

"I didn't say I had, Chief. Tosca could easily have decided there wasn't any danger because your friends didn't know Wilson was here."

There was a brief silence before Mike turned back to Pibble.

"We've agreed to differ," he said a little stiffly. "Ted's angle— and I don't blame him for it—is that one of Tosca's girls shot him. He may be right, but I've invested a lot in Wilson, and I can't take any risks . . . and somehow it doesn't feel like a straightforward lovers' bust-up."

"It doesn't to you. It does to me," said Cass, irritation getting the better of subservience.

In the suddenly claustrophobic atmosphere of the Incident Room (so absurdly more comfortable and convenient than most such camping-grounds, with its deep carpet and its warmth and privacy) Pibble could feel the case going sour over this dispute. A little more pushing from Mike, and Cass might become obsessed with proving that one of the nurses had fired the shots, however many Blue Bear hit-men might have left their footprints in the grounds that night. A moment of panic prickled at the base of

Pibble's spine. He exorcised it by summoning up the image of
Colonel McQueen paddling in the never-never wavelets. Cass had
got to be wrong. That was now an axiom.

"He was shot in the back of the head," he murmured.

"Yes," said Mike. "We've thrashed that out. It's almost the
only point Ted will concede . . ."   .

"Right," said Cass. "But I've been thinking. With all those A-
levels in the martial arts he had, it might be the only way she could
get him, sneaking up behind him."

"That's stretching it," said Mike. "You find somebody shot
close range in the back of the head like that, nine times out of ten
it's a gang killing."

"And one time out of ten it isn't."

Mike shrugged.

"Besides," said Cass, "whoever it was hung around a bit and
then turned him over."

"Check if he was dead."

"I thought these were professionals we were talking about. If
they aren't sure, they just put another bullet in, don't they? But
what I can see is one of the girls here—one of the nurses, for
preference—shooting him, then having a few minutes hysterics,
then calming down and nipping back to see if she'd really done it."

Mike restrained some retort and turned to Pibble.

"Anything else, Jimmy?"

"I don't know . . . routine . . . Tosca's sort of vanity . . . you'd
think he'd prefer to disrupt the existing routine, just to show who
was boss. Make them do things his way instead of fitting in with
theirs."

"Maybe. Where does that take us?"

"Well, suppose he knew that something was being planned
against Wilson . . ."

"I get you. If the Blue Bear lads, or whoever, knew his routine
then they could jump him and tie him up and it'd look quite
natural. But if they didn't know his movements, and still got him,
that might look as if George Tosca allowed himself to be got . . .

and wait a minute, they'd have to meet, here on the ground, to set it up efficiently. They might have had somebody here that night . . . What do you think, Ted?"

"Pretty airy-fairy. Besides, if Tosca was bent, from their point of view that's an asset. You don't go bumping your assets off."

"A quarrel," suggested Pibble.

"Possible," said Crewe. "Some of the Blue Bear lot are on a permanent high. You certainly couldn't say they were predictable."

"You've got no evidence Tosca was bent, even," insisted Cass.

"Oh, I think so. It rang a bell. It's difficult, isn't it, Jimmy? You've got colleagues who give you a feeling. Nothing you can prove, nothing you can even guess at. What do you do? Even if you've got the powers, you can't go firing men on a hunch."

"I don't know. Hunches. I think Foyle was before your time, Mike."

"That's right. Did you know he'd died, Jimmy?"

"Died?"

"Last May, I think. In Sydney, anyway. Ran a security firm there. Did very well—must have been getting on for a millionaire. I expect he managed to hang on to a lot of his loot from the Smiths, to set it up with. You didn't know?"

"I got a letter from him soon after he came out. I didn't open it."

"I gather he was something special. What about him?"

"Ur? Oh, nothing. He had hunches."

"I've got a bit of a hunch, young James . . ." And there'd be a warehouse full of silk stockings, traceable to some job. Or perhaps there wouldn't, but next time . . . an extended line of men in regulation capes moved slowly across a marshy wilderness, poking with long poles into ponds and quags; a shout in the drizzle-spinning wind, and a raised arm; the line coalescing round that centre, so that Pibble had to push his way between slithery capes to look down at the objet trouvé—a white curio, abstract, intricately patterned . . . Blink, and it was a human arm, once part of the entity which had

99

*thought of itself as Duggie Canino. The pattern of razor-cuts was
the first indication of what had been done to Duggie before he died.
Done, rumour said, by the Smiths with their own hands. Found,
rumour began to say, because the Smiths wanted people to know
what would happen to men who tried to play along with the Sicilian
interests which were beginning to move into London. "I've a bit of a
hunch, young James. Look at this map. The Ford with the blood-
stains here. Shooting incident here. Now, this route . . . they
wouldn't take a straight line, would they? So be a good lad and run a
search of this bit of waste, will you? Tell you what, if you find
anything, you can have the credit." But . . . there wasn't time . . . not
to do what they'd done to the man. Somebody was dragging a sack
of something out of a drainage ditch. A constable had begun to
vomit. Pibble stood among the faintly creaking capes, staring down
at the large pale limb reticulate with slashes, and knowing now
consciously what he had known unconsciously for five months, that
there was something too good to be true about Richard Foyle.
Another man was noisily sick. You can have the credit.*

"Any good?" said Cass, not very interested.

"Ur?"

"The chappie's hunches?"

"Too good. That's how . . . forget it."

"But there was something else you wanted to say," observed
Mike. "About hunches?"

"I suppose so. I feel a bit stupid. But you've met Lady
Treadgold?"

"Have I not? She threatened to write to the Home Secretary.
She calls him by his first name. Go on."

"Well, she's spotted who Wilson is. Almost pure hunch, but she
did it."

"Will she keep it to herself?"

"She's got a friend called Bunty something who knows Mary
Lou Isaacs."

"You're joking!"

"No. She doesn't know that Mrs Isaacs is looking for Wilson.

She only wants to write to her friend Bunty to get her to check whether her hunch is right."

"God give me strength! It could be true—Mary Lou started trying to get into nobby society a few years back—this Bunty woman might even be on the files . . ."

"Jaques. Bunty Jaques, I'm almost certain."

"Thanks. I can't say it's a help. Quite the opposite, but I suppose it's better to know than not to know."

"There's one thing might keep her quiet," said Pibble. "This is the stupid bit. She wants you to investigate the death of a resident here, some time late last year. Sir Archibald Gunter."

"Oh, no!" said Mike. "That's what she was on about, with her friend the Home Sec, I suppose. She didn't get round to details."

"I'm sorry," said Pibble.

"Doesn't the old bag realise—"

"Hang on," said Cass, quietly. "Has she got anything more, Mr Pibble? The inquest on Gunter was on December 4th."

Mike tilted his chair on to one leg and swung himself round to look at Cass. As far as Pibble was aware, Cass had produced the date out of the air, without referring to any kind of note.

"We had a letter," said Cass. "Anonymous. We're used to that; there's eleven of these places in our area—nothing as plushy as this, of course—and we keep getting letters from them, telling us that some old bird didn't pop off entirely by accident. Just what you'd expect, uh? The boredoms and the jealousies, for a start. Plus a feeling that death—*my* death—ought to have a meaning. Oughtn't to be an accident, if you follow. So when it gets right up close and people are dropping off all round, I start trying to make them into non-accidents. Something somebody's been doing a-purpose, uh?"

"I live here," said Pibble.

"There was something different about the Gunter letter?" asked Mike.

"Not that you'd notice. Our routine is to pay a friendly call, and it doesn't take more than an afternoon to find out who wrote 'em. Depending on circumstances, we give the old dear a gentle lecture and let it go at that. But this one, it wasn't any of the residents or nurses. The graphologist said it was an elderly woman using her normal handwriting and copying it out. He couldn't say whether it was just a fair copy of her own rough, or someone else's. A psychoboffin we got in had an interesting line. He said it was an absolutely routine poison pen—too routine, in fact. One or two bits came straight out of text-books."

"Tosca," said Pibble.

Mike tilted again, and swivelled back. Cass, while he spoke, had gradually recalled his limbs from their off-duty sprawl and was beginning to hunch into his pouncing posture.

"Lady Treadgold told me that Tosca had hinted that there was something phoney about Gunter's death," Pibble explained. "Her theory is that someone has been taking lump-sum, tax-free payments to knock off relatives who might linger on until the heirs' expectations came to nothing. She thinks Tosca found out and was blackmailing the someone."

"So the someone shot him?" said Mike, only half-mocking.

"Not necessarily. In her theory he was blackmailing everybody he could get any dirt on. He had the same shape of ears as a blackmailer she knew in Monte Carlo in the twenties. I'm sorry."

"Let's go back a bit," said Mike. "Ted, did you come up with anything smelly about that inquest?"

"Not a whiff. But remember this is a hospital."

"Jesus, yes. Hospitals. I heard something a couple of years back, Jimmy, which sounds like a bit of soap opera. An anaesthetist told me, at one of the city dinners I sometimes have to go to. One of the big teaching hospitals—he wouldn't say which. There was this up-and-coming surgeon, handsome, smooth, all that. World waiting for his scalpel. Vistas of millionaires lining his future. Then things went wrong. His operations didn't work any more. People died. You get the picture? Career almost in ruins. Hospital hushing things up the usual way. And then, quite by accident, it comes out that it wasn't his fault at all. Or not directly. He'd been having a real wow of an affair with one of his theatre nurses, and then he'd given her the push. But he hadn't sacked her from her job, because she was good at it. Does she bite the dust, have hysterics, call the Medical Council to witness to her wrongs? Not a bit of it. All she does is, quietly, without telling anyone, set out to ruin his career. See that his ops go wrong. See that his patients die . . . Makes your blood run cold, doesn't it?"

"What happened?"

"Oh, nothing. The hospital just kept on hushing things up. They posted the nurse up to Birmingham, and told the surgeon to confine his attentions to ward nurses in future."

"Do you think it was true?"

"Well, the bloke who told me had been doing his stuff with the claret. He rang me up next morning to make a point of telling me it was a well-known hospital chestnut. I found a theatre nurse from St Nigel's who'd been posted to Birmingham and committed suicide a few months later. I got a man to look through the death-certificates in the months before she went and found a sudden bump in one surgeon's failure rate. He's in America now. Point is, even inside the hospital, it only came out by accident. So what chance would there've been of our getting on to it? Ted's right, of course—the letters he gets all come from old biddies with nothing better to do—but there's the other side, too. When we run into a sort of villainy we're not geared to cope with, there's always the temptation to behave as if it didn't exist. I don't think I'm going to take this idea very seriously, but . . . What do you think, Ted?"

"Um. Just about worth seeing if we can get a lead through Tosca on who wrote that letter."

"He was a collector," said Pibble. "He'll have keepsakes."

"Plenty of those," said Cass. "But not from dear old ladies."

"Lady Treadgold thought he was ready to have a go at her."

"Naughty old bag."

"No. It's possible. I think he liked power."

"I know the sort," said Mike. "Rather have a woman who

103

didn't want him than one who did. Interesting what your psychoboffin said about the letter coming out of text-books, Ted. Tosca would have seen those."

"I think he would tell the actual writer that it was police work," said Pibble. "Something about trying to force a suspect into action. She would have to keep it secret, of course. Has he got a mother?"

"Yes," said Mike. "Very cut up, poor thing. She had his career all planned for him. I don't think I've seen her writing."

"Oh, I doubt it would be her, but she might recognise the writing."

"Haven't got it here," said Cass, "but it's still on file. I'll see to it."

"Fine. Anything else, Jimmy?"

"No. I don't think so. Not unless you've found my hat."

"Hat!" said Cass and Mike together.

"Must have blown off," mumbled Pibble, already preparing his seedy defences—those hopeless barricades of burnt out cases and other senile rubbish behind which the last ragged armies of freedom try to repel the storm-troopers.

"Wind," he added, as if attempting to pile that swirling pother on to his ramparts. Slowly he realised that the storm-troopers were failing to attack, distracted by some other interest. In fact Cass got up and left the room, coming back with three plastic bags.

"Stupid of us not to think of it," he said, drawing a shapeless dark lump from one of them. "Somehow, I hadn't pictured you wearing a hat. This it?"

Pibble took the object and stared at it, full of vague wonder, like a mother gazing at some tanned veteran and still managing to recognise her child who had marched off for the wars as a downy-chinned stripling all those years ago.

"Yes, that's it," he said. "Thanks."

It was all he could do not to put it on his head and see if it still fitted.

"Thick. Thick. Thick," said Cass, angrily.

"Not your fault," said Mike. "After all, it looked as if it had been in that bush for a year and a half. The shoes are different. Tell us what you think about this, Jimmy. It's your sort of thing."

A little dazed now, from the long effort of concentration, and the curious collapse of morale that followed the discovery that his barricade was not going to be attacked after all, Pibble gazed at the shiny, neat shoes which Cass was taking out of the other bag. Both pairs were black, one stout, with laces, the other flimsier and with elastic sides.

"They're small," he said.

"Seven and a half," said Cass. "At least Tosca was no flat-foot. The pair with laces was in the tower room with the rest of his duty clothes—quite stout, bad-weather shoes. Looks as though he'd gone to the tower in them and changed into his fancy gear when he got there—they had damp soles. The other pair's more interesting. He kept a lot of clothes, including about ten pairs of shoes. Sergeant Astley picked these ones out because they had damp soles, too. They've got that crackly feel, as if he hadn't worn them much. A few of his prints on them but the boffins say there's a microscopic scum of dust on top of the prints, which makes it look as if they've been sitting around some time since he last handled them."

"Two ways of looking at it," said Mike. "Plain or fancy. Plain is my way. Tosca wore them earlier because he didn't mind getting them wet. Picked them out of his cupboard the way you do; finger and thumb holding inside the two insteps. His socks would wipe those prints off soon as he was wearing them. Because they were wet he scuffed them off with his feet when he came in and slid them on to the shelf with his toes, save bending. All perfectly natural. Ted?"

"I go along with all that. There are marks on the heels where they were scuffed off. Only difference is that I don't think it was Tosca wearing them. A woman could, too, though she might clump a bit, and then she'd leave the right kind of prints in the tower."

"That makes it premeditated," said Mike. "And she'd still have to have a key to Tosca's room."

"OK, it was premeditated. I've felt it was all along. It's got that smell about it. Some bint went out to kill him—someone he'd had a go with and was moving on from. And I can't see why she shouldn't have a key to his room—he'd have to have given her one key already to get out of the house with, so why shouldn't he have given her two?"

Pibble recognised the tone of the argument as one that had been gone through many times before, now with an extra edge because they were in a sense appealing to him. Himself, he was beginning to feel the familiar shrivelling and withdrawal into a half-private world. For the moment the shoes obsessed that world. They had an inscrutable look, as though they held messages which they had no intention of delivering.

"How many?" he murmured.

"Come again," said Cass.

"Had he . . . moved on from, I mean?"

"Don't know for certain. We've got five, so far. There's three that don't mind talking about it. They're the sleeping-around sort. You can't see them getting jealous. Two more I've found who'll admit it, reluctantly—got their names out of the first three. That's all anyone knows about, but he was a fairly secretive operator."

"Five out of twelve is a fair score," said Mike.

"Did he take them to the tower?" asked Pibble.

"No," said Cass. "Two of them he took off for weekends. He had the use of the Jag, remember. But mostly he used his own room. He'd come and fetch them with his pass-key after he'd done his final rounds. You're right about his general attitude. The easy-going ones—the first three—said he was a pretty aggressive lover, and he tired of them (they didn't put it like that) after the first two or three days. The other two, I got the impression the affair lasted quite a bit longer, and he was quite considerate to begin with. It

106

was only when he'd got them trained, so to speak—come when he whistled, beg, lie down, all that—that he got bored."

"But he didn't give any of them keys," Mike insisted.

"Not that we know. But suppose he'd really set his heart on laying the whole lot. He'd start with the easy ones, and treat them like dirt. With the-not-so-easy he'd have to give 'em a bit more, act the gentleman some of the time. But when he got round to the real resisters, he would have to play things their way, give what he didn't want to give, and so on."

"You may be right," said Mike. "I must say I can't see a man of Tosca's type letting anybody into his room when he wasn't there. I'm not laying that down as a certainty—I'm long past believing you can predict how anybody else will actually behave, however well you know them—but he strikes me as the kind who wants his own secret nest where he can sit and gloat."

Pibble was barely listening by now. His vision was blurry with weariness, but the shoes glowed in the mist like the metallic carapaces of beetles assembled, pair and pair, to mate . . . Jenny . . . Tosca . . . He was perfectly aware that Jenny—*his* Jenny—was a construct. He knew her only from the angle which their relationship permitted and therefore his idea of her contained elements for which he had no proof and had moulded from an amalgam of guess and wish. One of these guess-wishes was that she, too, valued the relationship, and consciously or unconsciously chose to conform to the construct, while she was with him. By doing so, of course, she lessened the certainty even of his proofs, leaving yet larger spaces in which other Jennies—other people's constructs—could co-exist with his. But all these Jennies were not different people, they must all relate more or less to a "real" Jenny, and that meant that there were certain constructs which were incompatible with each other, which could not both be true. For instance, though her sexual experience was not in Pibble's knowledge—she had never said anything about it and spoke of other people's amours reluctantly, and with an almost comic dryness—it was inconceivable that in anyone else's con-

107

struct she was a girl who "slept around". It was not inconceivable that she had had a lover, or lovers, but it was inconceivable that she should accept a man like Tosca in that role.

And yet she must have been on Tosca's list, because he'd told Wilson it included all the nurses. He would have regarded her as a challenge. What ways could he have found of putting pressure on her? Something. She had been out that night, almost certainly to the tower. How had he persuaded her to go? Some hold, some leverage. And then, if he had that leverage, why should he not use it further? Pibble's mind refused to make the image. Instead there came to him another part of his Jenny-construct, a guess, but as sharp as proof. If Tosca had the leverage he would use it, and if he used it, Jenny would try to kill him.

Voices beyond the door. Her laugh.

"Wake up, Jimmy. Keeper's come."

He wanted to tell Mike that he was awake, fully aware, eager to help, able to put the whole investigation on to its right lines, but the room seemed to float round him and his mouth would only mumble meaninglessnesses. Jenny was there, not floating, quite close, arms akimbo, in mockery of her own real indignation.

"You wicked old man," she said. "Sneaking about again without telling me."

"He's been a great help," said Mike placatingly. "I'm afraid we've tired him out rather."

"Which of you is Doctor Watson, then?" she said. "Can you stand, Jimmy, or shall I get a wheelie?"

Mumble mumble. Statutory effort to rise. Sense of the blackness hovering close above. Her arm round his shoulders, hand against right ribs. Now. He rose, both sets of muscles working in easy tune, as if he and Jenny were dancing partners, into the darkness. He felt his lips beginning to smile as it closed down, happy in the confidence that she would hold him steady till it cleared.

The shoes, two pairs, gleaming still like beetles, came into focus.

108

They seemed at last to reveal their message. He turned to Mike.

"He took them off to paddle," he said urgently.

"Who?"

"Colonel McQueen."

Seven

DRIFTING AS IF on air the wheeled stretcher slid along the corridors. A lift absorbed it with a sigh like bliss and released it with another. Though the stretcher was in fact being pushed by an impassive young giant called Kerry, behind whom Jenny followed, Pibble's sense of them was merely a whiteness at the fringe of vision. Silence and smoothness made the journey seem involuntary, as though Pibble were a particle of food being passed, with two attendant digestive amoebae, along the shining guts of Flycatchers. The building itself became a chambered cell inhabited by a life-system whose metabolism sucked into it decaying fragments of humanity, absorbed their monetary juices, and excreted the remains into cemeteries and crematoria. The creature lived by death, but death of another kind had got into its system, and now the creature itself was sick. Elsewhere in its vague vitals Cass and his men moved like other corpuscles, summoned to isolate and destroy the invader. But the creature itself continued to suck in, digest, excrete, and as a part of the digestion process, Pibble was now on his way to a nerve ganglion, Doctor Follick's so-called surgery.

There was a wait in the ante-room. Jenny came round and touched his cheek.

"Not too tired after this morning?" she whispered.

He mumbled, hardly noticing, lost in a mind-wandering vision of another great sick creature, the thing that had inhabited

Norman Shaw's grimed and ponderous building by the Thames. Scotland Yard, where Pibble had spent half his working life, had been a creature of the same order as Flycatchers, but enormously more complex. It lived not on death but on the sickness of society, and its complexity made it capable of a dim sort of self-awareness which manifested itself mainly as hypochondria—endless inspection of its own body for traces of the diseases by which it lived. Perhaps all creatures which have to present to the world a face of glorious health tend to brood in private on the latest throb of a neck-muscle or the new-found patch of numbness below the hip; but Pibble had been a corpuscle himself in that body when the genuine disease had taken hold, and then in slime and pain the creature had begun to digest itself. To passers-by along the Embankment the solemn old building had appeared unchanged, had remained both reassuring and menacing; but internally there had been chaos, sudden scurryings, messages from the nerve-ends misrouted and distorted, clottings of cells in curious places, whole organs suddenly functionless. There had taken place a near-collapse of the life-system, much like that which Pibble's own body had undergone in the last few months.

Perhaps it was the memory of the Foyle inquiry that made Pibble, even in his semi-trance, conscious as soon as he was at last drifted into the surgery that this visit, though a routine part of the Flycatcher creature's metabolism, was at the same time an incident in its sickness. The awareness faded as he roused himself to cope with his role as patient, but never quite vanished.

When Pibble had first visited the surgery he had been past noticing much more than it seemed to have a remarkable amount of equipment in it. Later, as his mind improved, he assumed that the display was mainly there to impress the patient, to imply that his fees were being spent on all that was latest and most fashionable by way of geriatric miracle; even to hint that when the old heart finally faltered, or the old spleen ceased to do whatever it was spleens did, Toby Follick would fetch out from a cabinet some chrome and plastic knick-knack which would take over the functions of exhausted flesh and begin another whole lifetime. There was still some truth in that picture—no doubt it was why Follick's employers had sanctioned the expenditure—but it was also now apparent that Follick needed the gadgets as much for his own sake as his patient's. They gave him the same kind of thrill of possession that a roomful of netsuke or Tang grave-ornaments might give a collector of such stuff. They fed his self-image as the super-competent healer, but they also fed Pibble's image of him as the comic conjurer, on stage now, surrounded by glittering cabinets into which bowls of goldfish would disappear and be transformed into monstrous bouquets of plastic tulips.

Follick preferred to see his patients on stretchers, even when they were well enough to walk. There was no comfortable chair in the large, light room, and Maisie perched on a stool to take down any notes or instructions. The thin whine of dust-extractors filled the room, and a tall grey cabinet against the inner wall blinked a few lights on and off, apparently at random. The sense of a life being lived at Flycatchers, of which the patients and staff were only cellular parts, was especially strong in the surgery.

"Well, what have you been up to since I last saw you?" said Follick. "Exploring the Orinoco?"

"Ur."

"He got himself up this morning," said Jenny, speaking through the filter of discipline. "His room was empty. I found him down in the offices, talking to his friends."

"Did you now? Did you now?" said Follick, apparently delighted by the surprise.

"He was a bit tired after that, but he's had a rest since. He had a couple of low days, like you said he would, but he started picking up yesterday."

"Fine, fine. Let's have a look at the documents."

Follick moved out of Pibble's line of vision, so he lay quiet, not thinking of anything much, until his eye was caught by Maisie. There was an oddity about her pose as she too waited, a tension which she was trying to disguise by lolling, as far as the stool

112

allowed her. He thought she was deliberately avoiding his eye until he realised that the target of her non-attention must be Jenny.

She straightened but at the same time relaxed as Follick muttered a snatch of jargon for her to take down. Jenny came into Pibble's line of sight to peel off his blanket. Ritual apparently demanded that this task should be done by the acolyte, but that the priest himself must remove the final veil, the examination shift which was the only garment patients wore for these encounters. Follick performed the rite and began to press Pibble's flesh with an abstracted air, like a man in a supermarket pressing a Camembert to see if it is ripe, while most of his mind is on the young mum in the tight yellow jersey who is leaning over the cooler cabinet to compare butter prices.

"These abrasions and contusions are healing, Jenny?"

"Yes, slowly. They still hurt him a bit."

"Quite a bit, I should think, if he got himself up this morning and went on the gad."

"He walked back to his room without a wheel-chair. I didn't help him much."

"Um. Tell me, Jimmy—this is a medical question and not bloody inquisitiveness—why did you do that? Just for a gossip?"

"No. Something I wanted to . . ."

"And did it hurt?"

"A bit. Sore, not proper pain."

"Right . . . you see, what I'm getting at is this. In a sense I oughtn't to be treating you, because I'm a geriatrician, and you're not old enough for me. Apart from the atherosclerosis in your legs you aren't beyond late middle age. Your eyesight and hearing are better than most people's, your muscular co-ordination is fine, you're continent, your heart's in reasonable nick, and so on. As I've told you before, it's all a question of getting the blood to the brain. Now, we've been talking as though your problem was that you had low blood-pressure, and in a sense that's true. On the other hand I could show you plenty of medical text-books which say there's really no such condition as low blood-pressure."

"Uh?"

"It occurs, of course. It's quite common—in cases of shock, for instance. But it doesn't go on and on, an illness in its own right. One way of describing your case is that you are in a permanent state of mild shock. Right? Of course this wasn't apparent when you first came in because you'd run yourself down so far, but now we've had a chance to sort you out . . . Let me make a guess. Some time about eighteen months ago, or perhaps a bit more, something happened which stopped you in your tracks. . . ."

Mary's face, the colour of dirty snow on the glistening pillow. The coffin on the crematorium chute, the twiddling organ music, the chute empty. He hadn't even seen her go.

"All right, you don't have to tell me what it was. But listen, if you've followed what I've been saying, you'll see that there's a limit to what we can do for you, and we've about reached it. Pills and comfort can take you this far, but from now on it's going to be up to you—it's going to be up to your moral energy, your will-power. I haven't talked to you about this before, because, to be frank, I didn't think you had it in you. But since last Thursday I've changed my mind. You can do it if you want to, and in that case I think I can help you a bit more. With your co-operation I want to try a little experiment."

"Ur?"

"A little experiment," repeated Follick, brown eyes glistening, as if the phrase were a magical formula with which he proposed to conjure up the spirit of healing. "Crank him up to semi-recumbent, will you, Jenny. Maisie, will you hook up the encephalograph and the cardiograph, and then if both of you wouldn't mind waiting out in the ante-room . . . Maisie, I'm not taking any calls for half an hour . . . that's high enough, Jenny . . . now, I'm going to tape a few terminals on . . . there . . . and there . . . . cover him up, Jenny . . . and you hold this in your right hand . . . grip it firmly and don't let go . . . and finally there's the hat . . . um. . . not too tight? Great. Thanks, Maisie. Thanks, Jenny."

Pibble felt oddly detached, a mere spectator of Follick's bustling and eager performance. The rubbery terminal he had been given to grip, the absurd little padded skull cap with its moon-man cables snaking out of it, which Follick had shown him before adjusting it to nestle on his scalp, the glossy gadgetry, Follick's own almost factitious joy in the employment of his toys—all these seemed such obvious precursors of a trick which wasn't going to work—or was going to work in the way the performer least expected. Pibble watched him cross to the wall and press a switch in one of the cabinets. A small but very intense white light blazed into being. Follick came back and vanished behind the stretcher. There was a thump and a rustle. Pibble bent his neck, rolled his eyes up to their limit, and found himself staring straight up two dark nostrils. He deduced that Follick had perched himself on Maisie's stool at the stretcher head.

"Don't look at me, James. I want you to concentrate on that light over there. Try not to look at anything else. Grip that terminal a little tighter. Concentrate on the light."

Follick's voice changed, becoming deeper and quieter, without any emphasis at all, but despite the flatness suffused with a steady energy as he repeated and repeated his instructions. The light swam and floated in greeny blackness, an obsessing glare. There was nothing else in the world except the light and the dull, insinuating drone.

"Good. And now your heart is going to beat a little faster. A little faster. Don't think about it. Just look at the light. Good. You heart is beating a little faster. Good. Tell me about your mother now."

Mamma, thin and straight, stalking away along the pavement in a black, ankle-length dress and the curious little hat which marked her out as a Saint of the Revised Chapter. Jimmy, not quite eighteen, leaning against the low brick wall of the front garden and watching her in a muddle of pity and guilt and irritation, aware that during the course of their short and almost wordless quarrel about whether he should go with her to Chapel he had finally decided to apply to join

115

the police cadets.

"Good. Good. Keep the heart steady. Steady. Now you are going to raise your blood-pressure just a little. Raise your blood-pressure. You can do it. Raise your blood-pressure. Keep your heart steady. Steady. Watch the light. The light. Now tell me about this shot you heard."

Shooting gallery at Hendon. Instructor stripping automatics in front of a small, bored class, Pibble somewhere in the middle of them. Glare of lamps on concrete. Faint smell of fine oil and fainter still of burnt powder. Concrete dust and boredom the main atmosphere. From the gallery proper the unsystematic crack of shots fired at moving targets. One shot, and all was changed. Light and smells the same but now the boredom was something else. The instructor paused in mid sentence, laid down his weapon, turned to the padded door, opened it, stared, shut it. Why had they all known? How had the communal shudder begun even before the instructor had turned from the bench? Had the sound differed physically when the cadet who had been practising (blond, acne-speckled, enormous) had put his pistol against the roof of his mouth and fired that last shot? The questions continued to ache long after the equal mystery of why the young giant had suddenly felt compelled to die had ceased to seem to matter.

"Good. Good. Keep your heart steady. Watch the light. Steady. Steady. Keep your blood-pressure up. Good. Good. Now tell me about the shot you heard five nights ago, when you were in your room at Flycatchers."

The voice, even as it asserted the need for steadiness, had faltered slightly. Something—frustration, or fear, or merely inattention—had caused a crack in the dull surface. Till that moment Pibble's world had been filled with the light and the voice, but through the fissure a tiny wisp of consciousness escaped. He was aware that he had been using his throat-muscles, aware that he was under some kind of pressure from which there was no escape, physical or mental, in the present. Refuge lay in the past, in childhood, in the years of health. This wisp of free conscious-

116

ness moved his lips.

"Don't know."

"You found a body, you remember?"

Tall blind house, up by the railways. The neighbours silent in doorways, ominous presences, like trees. The man at the door, bare torso, pyjama trousers; muscular, unsurprised. "Bit of a dust-up with the missus, Sarge. Nothing special." His whitish eyes flickering to the street and back. Silence of June dusk. More watchers now, and nearer. Whose side . . .

"We'll just come in and have a word with her, sir, if you don't mind. Have a look out in the garden, Jim my lad. That yell come from somewhere at the back. Hey! No, you don't! . . ."

Two in the morning. Sergeant Stacker's tall brow gleaming in the office gas light. "Can't expect that sort of excitement every time you go out on the beat, my lad. They'd known all along, those neighbours, but it's not the sort of street goes talking to coppers." Telephone tinkle. "Hello. Hello. Yes . . . If I weren't a religious man . . . Thanks for letting me know. Jim, my boy, they've found another pit in the garden. Three more, and not one of them ten years old. That makes nine . . . and if I hadn't been showing you round the manor . . ." Stacker fatherly, solemn, doing his best to reassure the new recruit, but himself shaken, shaken . . .

"Good. Good. Slow your heart-beat a little. It's too fast. Slower. Slower. Good. Blood-pressure up. Up. Good. Good. Watch the light. The light. The light. Now I want you to forget everything that happened before you came to Flycatchers. Forget everything before you came to Flycatchers. Watch the light. Forget everything before you came to Flycatchers."

The crack was wider now; wider not because of any further irresolution in the voice, but because of a rebellion inside Pibble against the command, a command, effectively, to cease to be. He was what had happened to him before he came to Flycatchers. Time since then had been a vacuous after-life. No! He watched the light still, but was aware of himself watching it. He heard the voice, but was conscious of its being Doctor Follick's voice. And

117

Jenny was waiting in the ante-room . . .

"Watch the light. You've let your heart-beat slow. Faster a little. Faster. And your blood-pressure. Raise it. Raise it. Good. Good."

It was important to accept the voice, to watch the light. The process was healing. There was some other reason . . . no matter. He let the light obsess him again, allowed the voice to become disembodied. But swimming down into these vaguenesses he clasped to himself that central No which he had clutched from the surface. He would not forget.

"Now tell me what Mr Crewe is thinking."

Mike is thinking about one of his girls, the Greek one, probably. Water rattles on the car roof, not because it is raining, but because the traffic is jammed under the as yet unfinished M4, whose construction seems to produce this drizzle. Pibble watches Mike smiling to himself, and feels that mixture of envy and contempt with which the sexually impacted confront the free-and-easy. A twitch of movement beyond Mike's profile, minute but characteristic. "Don't look for a moment, Mike. We've been recognised. Chappie in the Jaguar next to you. Can't put a name to him." Pause. Four men in the Jag seem interested in something further over. Mike twists, winds down window, adjusts wing mirror. Jam moves. "I think I know the chappie in the back, sir. Difficult from that angle, but it might be Dicey Martin." "Sure?" "No." "Still, they knew who we were, I think." "Yes, sir. Sergeant Colnaghi was saying something in Mess last week about Dicey Martin getting ready to pull a big one." "Colnaghi's in Serious Crime isn't he? Like to stop and give him a ring? We've got ten minutes to spare. Let them get away first . . ." Which was how Martin and five others were picked up halfway through the Heathrow Bullion Raid, and how Mike Crewe got his file moved into the Rapid Promotion sector.

"Good. Good. Keep your heart-beat there. Steady. Steady. Raise the blood-presure. Raise the blood-pressure. Watch the light. Steady. Steady. Forget what happened to you before you came to Flycatchers. Can you forget it? Can you forget it?"

118

No! yelled the mind, but the drugged lips merely mumbled the dimmest of negatives.

"Very well. Now keep the heart-beat steady. We're doing fine. The blood-pressure is up a little. Keep it there. Keep it there. You are going to practise raising your blood-pressure three times a day, at nine, two and seven in the evening. Three times a day. Nine, two, and seven. You will practise. Now you can relax, relax. Good. In a minute I will switch off the light and you can wake up. Relax. Relax. Now tell me how much you know about what is going on."

"That's the sickening thing about our job, young James. If you're any good, you get to know what happened, more often than not. Like a traffic cop, you can look at the skid-marks. But that's all past history. What wouldn't you give to know a bit of present history? Tell me frankly, young James, how much do you know about what's going on?" A slight lowering of the voice was enough to change the emphasis of the last sentence. Beyond the partition the clientele of the Seven Stars boomed bonhomie. Dickie's glance, intent but mocking; his wallet out as if to begin ordering a fresh round; Dickie casually letting it fall open . . .

Light became dark.

". . . tenners, the old sort," a voice was saying. "A great mound of them, half a year's pay. He was letting me see them on purpose."

The voice was Pibble's own, quiet but remarkably firm for the first few syllables, but then dwindling into a weary mumble. He stopped talking. The dark became the daylight of the surgery, with the ghost of that intense spot still swimming through it in greens and reds on the retina. Follick came round to where he could look down at the stretcher. The excitement was still there, mixed now with an air of baffled wonder. Another goldfish bowl had become a bunch of tulips, evidently.

"Sorry about that, James," he said. "I got a bit further in than I meant. You see the idea is to concentrate your physical attention on things like the light and the grip in your hand, and your mental

119

attention on mental events by getting you to talk. I lure the sentries out of the way, if you see what I mean, and that allows me to sneak in and plant a few suggestions into the autonomous nervous system while the normal control-levels are distracted. It'll be interesting to see if we get anywhere. You're quite a good subject for your age, you know. How much can you remember?"

"Not much . . . Like dreams . . . Dickie Foyle . . . Mike . . . Old Stacker . . ."

"Don't worry. That's why I sent the nurses out. It's all in absolute confidence."

"Ur."

"You're not too tired?"

"No. Feel as if I'd had a rest, lying here."

"Good. That's just how you should feel. Now, there's something else I'd like to have a word about, if you're up to it. It's not medical . . . In fact, I need your advice. Mr Brackley, one of our senior shareholders, gave me a ring this morning—doesn't normally happen, but they're getting a little jumpy, and they asked me . . . Tell me, do you know anything about a patient we have here called Wilson?"

"A little. He paid me a visit a few days back."

"Did he now? . . . Well, in that case . . . Look, obviously I can't expect you to tell me anything confidential. I'll just assume that you know as much about this Wilson chappie as I do—which since he's not my patient was nothing at all until Mr Brackley telephoned—and I rather gather from his tone that *he* hadn't really been told anything like the whole truth and if he had we wouldn't have taken Wilson on . . . You know we make a special feature of our security arrangements? That's the reason Mr Brackley got on to me—I do the liaison on the medical side . . ."

(Of course, thought Pibble. The electrically controlled shutters. A typical Follick gadget.)

"You see, people who really want that sort of service don't mind what they pay. But they've got to be sure it's working. A murder on the premises isn't a very good advertisement, but at least it was a security guard who was shot, and in some ways that's a plus—shows that the system is functioning, and that it's needed. We can cope with that. What's really worrying the owners now is having these troops of policemen all over the place, inside the building, getting nowhere as far as anyone can make out. That is very bad for morale, and in this sort of business, which depends so much on word-of-mouth, a few weeks' dissatisfaction can result in two or three years loss of profits. You follow?"

"You want to know how long the investigation will go on?"

"Yes."

"Can't say. If they don't solve the case, they won't close the file for a long time. Might still be a couple of officers working on it for a year."

"Here? At Flycatchers?"

"No. It's not only Tosca, it's Wilson. If they decide Tosca's death had no connection with Wilson, they'll concentrate on his other activities and probably clear it up in a couple of weeks, and you'll be rid of them after that. But of course that'll probably mean the arrest of somebody inside Flycatchers—not such a good advertisement. But if they find there was a Wilson connection, then the murderer's probably from outside, and they can investigate that just as well—better—from their own centres. But they'll want to keep a few chaps on here till they are pretty sure Wilson's safe."

"They won't take him away?"

"They might; depends whether they can find anywhere else as good. You'd know about that, more than I would."

"There's a couple of places . . . Thanks, James. I get the picture. I'll tell Mr Brackley. Now, let's get you unplugged."

Pibble lay still. He felt weary and relaxed, but remarkably well and clear-headed. He had positively enjoyed explaining the logical outcome of the police investigation, putting the sequence of events together in coherent sentences, instead of letting Follick fish sense out of a jumble of half-senile mutterings. He watched Follick remove the terminals and the moon-man hat, and then stride to the ante-room door and open it with a characteristic flourish, as though it was a cabinet from which he had triumphantly vanished the two nurses.

And replaced them with what? Just as characteristic as the door-opening was the suddenness with which the gesture stopped, unfinished, while the eyebrows rose in unashamed surprise at what the cabinet now contained. Maisie and Jenny came stiffly into the room, both flushed, and with Jenny's cap crooked and her hair (normally as neat in its natural curls as the orderly arrangement of scales on a mackerel) half-tousled. It looked as though Maisie had been crying. Kerry followed them into the room, his face transformed by a wide, vague grin which gave him a look of daft benevolence, like the bamboozled ogre in a folk-tale.

As the stretcher drifted back through the corridors, Pibble let his tiredness take hold. He slept, and only half-awoke when Kerry lifted him effortlessly across into his own bed. Familiar blankets closed around him. He heard the door whimper, click where the stretcher jarred it, and close. Fingers settled round his wrist and found the pulse.

"Sound as a bell," he murmured.

"Jimmy!"

He opened his eyes and saw her face above him, cap still awry, hair out of place.

"You're a patient," she said. "You're not allowed to play tricks on the staff. Only April the First."

"A ration of one trick will be issued to each patient . . . wasn't there a chap called Bertie Foster-something?"

Awake now, he was aware that something had happened during an earlier period of unconsciousness. Whatever it was left him with a sense of almost hysterical exhilaration, the aftermath of victory. The Old Guard, maimed, leaderless, marching with ancient muskets, had fought off a computerised modern army. Cracking good show, Pibble—pity you can't remember what the battle was about.

"Foster-Banks," she said. "He was frightful. He once put itching powder in all the wheel-chairs. His jokes weren't funny at all. We got up a deputation, saying that either he left or we did, but it wasn't any good. He turned out to be a big shareholder. One of the owners."

"What happened?"

"He died before it got that far."

"What they call a merciful release. Something's happened to your hair."

"I was fighting with Maisie."

"Uh?"

"She wouldn't let me listen at the door. Goodness, she's strong. Kerry just stood there grinning. I suppose it must have looked like a bit of a silent movie, me trying to get to the door and Maisie holding me against the wall and tears lolloping down her cheeks and neither of us saying a word."

"Why? . . ."

"You're my patient, aren't you? I have to know what's going on, and . . . it was almost as if he'd summoned up a devil or something—there was this strange voice going on and on; it took me ages to work out it must be you—and Maisie wouldn't let me listen! What on earth were you on about?"

"Don't know. He put me in a trance and made me talk. Idea is you make the mind distract itself, or something . . . when I came to I was telling him about Dickie . . . trying to bend me . . ."

"Don't try and tell me now. You're tired."

". . . Didn't bring it off . . ."

"I could see that."

"Uh?"

"It's a look men have. When they want something and they don't get it. I'm not blind!"

She let go of his wrist and swung away from the bed, snatching his pyjamas from the back of the chair and then standing irresolute, as if not sure why she was holding them.

"Jenny?"

123

"Yes!"

"Tosca. He wanted . . ."

She turned very pale, and then a raw and mottled blush suffused her face and glowed like a rash on her neck. Her mouth worked as though something glutinous were stuck to her teeth.

"Must know," he muttered.

She shut her eyes and deliberately controlled the fit. Paler than ever now, she bent her head as though she was studying the texture of his pyjamas.

"Yes, he did," she said in a flat voice. "And no, he didn't. If you ask me anything like that again, ever, however much you need to know, I shall leave and go somewhere else."

Pibble dozed the early evening away, physically and emotionally exhausted. Self-pity and boredom—pity for his boredom, boredom with his pity—wound through their endlessly reiterated reel. Jenny had left the radio on, but it remained gibble-gabble in his ears. The time-pips for the seven o'clock news seemed to break the trance, and though the news itself was nothing but strikes and bad-weather blues, he listened to it. When the loathed Archers followed, the stimulus was enough to make him switch the machine off, and simply lie, thinking, till supper came. His thoughts were not about himself, and surprised him by their coherence.

Eight

"ALMOST SUMMER," SAID Jenny over his shoulder.

"Don't you believe it. Springs are getting later and later."

"Look, those are going to be crocuses, aren't they?"

She stopped the chair so that he could inspect a few dark green spikes poking through the winter-withered turf.

"Yes," he said, "but they'll be looking just the same in six weeks' time."

"You're hopeless. I want it to be summer. You and I are going to win the mixed doubles."

"Who is there to beat?"

"Nobody, yet. They use the old tennis court as a croquet lawn. Colonel McQueen is the expert; he teaches all the new nurses to play. Makes sure we swing the mallet right; you know, lot of standing around with his hands over yours, adjusting your grip."

She laughed with mockery but without bitterness. The morning was deceptively soft and bright, but cold enough to make sitting still in the wheel-chair uncomfortable, despite gloves and scarf and overcoat.

"I'd like to walk for a bit," he said.

"Sure? I'm not certain you should be up, even, let alone out and tramping around."

"I'm all right."

She stopped the chair, helped him to his feet, put his stick into his right hand and drew his left over her shoulder.

"What are you smiling at?" she said.

The answer was McQueen, cunning old goat. But though the relationship seemed to have re-established itself uninjured, he wasn't going to risk stepping even that close to forbidden ground. He felt wide awake—had done, since soon after breakfast—and it was noticeable that when he had stood from the wheel-chair the customary darkness barely brushed its wing across his consciousness.

"Let's go and look at the scene of the crime," he said.

"Oh! You can't get up the tower—they've put a new lock on it."

"Never mind."

With Jenny pushing the empty chair they moved slowly, slantwise along the path across the shallow slope of lawn that spread down from the front of the house to the ha ha. The Downs, hummocked and shadowed, looked only half the distance away that they did on other days. Flycatchers rode its own swell of green in placid ugliness.

"You're quite right, its being like a ship," he said. "I thought of that when I was going out in the storm. Deck bucketing about, you know."

"You didn't!" she said. "That's extraordinary!"

"Ur?"

"Oh . . . just you thinking about it at a time like that, I suppose."

He had felt an instant of withdrawal, where his arm ran across her back, but she relaxed almost at once. He couldn't detect any sense of wariness or reluctance as they neared the colonnade.

"What are you looking for?" she said. "Scraps of thread's the usual thing, isn't it, or bits of tobacco ash?"

"The police will have found all those. They're the experts. It's a nuisance, sometimes, the stuff you find. I mean, look at these ramblers—any of you coming along here in one of your cloaks might catch a bit on a thorn. Look there. And there."

"Why do you think they'd be wearing a cloak?"

"You misunderstand me. I wasn't talking about that night in

126

particular. You're wearing a cloak now."

"They'd look like a bat, wouldn't they? He'd be watching from above— Countess Dracula, going to her tower."

"If that's what happened."

She glanced at him, a little surprised, and looked away. It was as though her dancing-partner had put a foot out of step. He was morally certain now that she had come out on the night of the storm, and almost as sure that she had been to the tower. What's more, she was aware of these certainties, tending only to over-estimate their strength and detail. He looked down at her small hand on the white rail of the chair.

"What size shoes do you take?" he said.

She laughed.

"I don't, or at least they don't make them. If they did they'd be three and a half Cs so I have to get them made—my feet are almost square, like a boxer pup's. Sometimes, I think that the factory didn't quite finish making me. Look."

She held up her other hand to show him its square, muscular palm and its extraordinarily short fingers.

"I know," he said. "This must about be where I fell over. I crawled the rest of the way. I wonder if it was me broke that clematis."

"Look, it's growing," she said, pointing at the juicy leaf-buds in the axils of the wizened foot of stem.

"They start very early. I wonder how much he could actually see from up there . . ."

He turned at the tower door and faced along the colonnade. It was a continuation of the terrace that ran the whole length of the house, which meant that the tower was set a little forward from the line of the building. A marksman up there would be in a classic enfilade position.

"Which is Mr Wilson's window, do you know?" he said.

"He's got the corner room, that one there. One window looks this way and the other one out front. He always likes these curtains drawn before it's dark; in fact, since George died he's left

127

them shut all day."

Her tone implied that these were facts he needed to know. He stood pondering, conscious of her support and the layer of extra warmth where the hem of her cloak had half-wrapped itself round his trouser leg. Countess Dracula. *"I wish I knew why Mr X needed a bodyguard."* That was after the shooting. Had Tosca told her, or had she worked it out? And when? Suppose she'd known before the shooting, surely she'd have mentioned it during her endless speculations on Wilson's role. The knowledge hadn't been dangerous then. And if she hadn't known, that must mean she could not have planned Tosca's death. She'd need to know about the gun. A previous visit? Several? No. Last evening's outburst surely meant that Tosca had made an attempt to cross her off his list, and failed. It could even seem to mean that he'd failed because she'd shot him; to judge from her reaction to Pibble's question, she was capable of that. He considered her last visit on the evening of the murder, with her hair glistening from its wash and her presence humming with life and energy—even that could be accounted for as an exhilaration of triumph over the dragon—but it was a single event, out of context.

During the last few days before that, when Pibble's own plan had been complete and he'd only needed to wait for a night of storm, he had become almost painfully sensitive to her fluctuations of mood, and had perceived nothing. She'd had a distinct low a month or so before, but had emerged from it, and was normal, neither exhilarated nor depressed. If she had killed Tosca, it had been on impulse.

And that meant she hadn't killed him. The McQueen principle held firm. Something had definitely been planned to happen in the tower, by somebody other than Tosca. Perhaps the shooting had been only an accident, or by-product, but the element of calculation hung around, like the after-smell of cigars. Experience could smell it, and experience did not rely on hunches. The killer had taken thought, done sums . . . and the sums had gone wrong.

One of those steep South London streets, familiar from childhood.
Stained glass in porch windows; stucco-ed walls; raw-red tiles,
golden privet hedges round minute front patches. Reek of vomit
strong, even on pavement. In the dark hall passage appalling.
Almost glowing in that stench and gloom a freak of beauty, a
woman. Dead man in front parlour, face down in vomit. Classic
Victorian poisoning, sixty years late. Everything there—husband a
brute, lover a herbalist, and the woman, pale and statuesque, with
the classic oval face, and the crazed calm of misty-grey eyes.
Solicitor arrives with letter from husband, voicing his suspicions.
Arrests. Charges. Only mystery apparent smallness of dose to cause
all that agony; but then evidence that dead man ultra-sensitive to
hyoscine. Trial. Black cap. Sentence. What fluke decreed that a Mr
Bill Dudgeon, junk dealer, should pick out from a crate of unread-
able books, unbid-for in the sale, the Sermons of the Rev
W.W. Dudgeon, *and looking to see if the holy author was any*
relation, discover blank pages, filled with the dead man's secret
diary? All planned to punish wife with sentence of attempted murder.
Every clue planted. Dose calculated to the microscruple, except that
the dead man's doctor had never told him about his sensitivity. And
they'd hanged the lovers the morning Mr Dudgeon came into the
station with his find. All at the height of the first anti-hanging
campaign, too. But the desk-sergeant, a passionate pro-roper, had
found a kindred spirit in Mr Dudgeon, convinced him of the damage
his find would do to the cause, so Mr Dudgeon had taken it home and
put it in his stove.

"I don't think she ever realised what was happening to her,"
Pibble murmured aloud. "I hope not."

"So do I," said Jenny.

He turned to stare at her, and she nodded as if to show she'd
meant what she said.

"I've got to go in now," she said. "Or I'll be late with Lady
Treadgold's massage. Anyway I'm getting cold, and so are you.
Hop into the wheelie, Jimmy, and I'll run you back."

"All right."

Snared by the apparent well-being, the phantasmal euphoria he had felt after breakfast, Pibble had booked himself for lunch in the dining-room. Rather wishing he hadn't, he waited in the coffee room vaguely looking through the property advertisements—each an instant fantasy life—in an old copy of *Country Life*, and thinking without any real purpose about Wilson, the retired dragon, who moved as though his heart were the frailest of fine glass and was yet determined that his life should be prolonged into the prosecutions of his old acquaintances. Even if he was dead, they would remember him in their cells. Pibble found this longing alien; he himself wanted no sort of immortality. A year and a half ago, when he was starting on the downward slither, he had absent-mindedly taken a train from central London to the wrong home, not the room in Hackney but the undulating road in the south-east suburbs where he had lived for over thirty years, until Mary died. He had only recognised what he was doing when he turned the last corner and saw that his rose garden was gone, obliterated, the whole triangle chopped off to make room for a new roundabout. Standing there, blinking at the alteration, he had been mostly amazed that he felt no pang. The roses had been his pleasure, his satisfaction. Mary had admired them and approved of them out of her natural competitiveness—her James grew better blooms than anyone for a mile around—but Pibble never felt any of that. The roses existed for him and he for them, and if he was gone it was better that they should vanish too. He did not want even the ghost of a rose. And so with everything else, no shreds, no after-effects, no grave or headstone. If as he went he could have sucked away with him the memories a few remaining friends might have of him, he would have done so. That applied to Jenny too.

Was that true? For instance, half an hour ago he had felt a strong urge to try and tell her about the Balham poisoner going in her daze of beauty, innocent to the gallows. He was aware without thinking about it that this wish was partly defensive, an attempt to explain what he had been talking about, and so in a way undo Jenny's last remark, and thus not have to add it as an extra element into the by now tedious puzzle. But at the same time he acknowledged a sense of daily increasing solidity in himself, obviously connected with improving health but not the same thing. And this growing confidence in his own existence seemed in turn to be connected to the shocking energy of certain memories—things not thought of for many, many years—which nowadays would spring at him out of the apparent oblivion where they had been lying all the while in ambush. It was as though memory itself was trying to assert his existence. He had seen these sights, done these things. In a sense he was them. And if he was going, after all, to live, then so were they.

The door of the coffee room opened, and Pibble began to cringe a little. He had chosen the stuffy little nook because it was seldom used before meals, so he had hoped to enjoy an hour or so of unbraced privacy without having to struggle up to his own room. He glanced up to see what thickness of armour he was going to have to put on. Mrs Fowles, Flycatchers' general secretary, came in first, then held the door, beaming short-sightedly at the room and making a well-there-it-is gesture with her pudgy and bangle-rattling arm. The woman who stood just inside the door—Mrs Fowles was evidently showing a newcomer round—was a striking contrast, slim, short, dressed all in heavy black, severely smart, probably in her sixties. She held a black cane in one hand, but not in a manner that suggested she was used to needing it. Her skin had the slight transparency of recent illness. She nodded at the room, accepting it as adequate but unenthralling. As Mrs Fowles turned to go the newcomer's gaze met Pibble's.

Without realising it he had been staring. Perhaps the unconscious mind had a given signal that something out of the ordinary had happened, but now, before he could look decorously aside, recognition flashed from the woman's eyes. Her gaze swept past him unfaltering. With another nod she turned and followed Mrs Fowles out. The door closed.

Memory, of course, refused its task. It was like a Russian farmworker, hopelessly incompetent on the collective, allowing the crops to rot in the barns and the tractors to rust amid weed-riddled fields, but capable of raising record crops on his own small patch. Pibble was perfectly certain that he and the woman had met at some time, but equally unable to raise the faintest flicker of a notion where or when. Under his effort to recall her the whole of his memory apparatus began to sulk. At one point, in an effort to re-stimulate it, he returned to the Balham poisoning but found that even there both outline and detail had become shadowy. In the end he took refuge in the notorious inattention of the old and returned to doddering through *Country Life* until the soft throb of the gong announced lunch.

Energy continued to wane. Pibble ate at a table by himself, concentrating on his food with deliberate greed. Taste was a sense that seemed not to have diminished at all, and so could be asked to stand in for other vanished pleasures. The woman in black had attracted the attentions of Colonel McQueen, who must have invited himself to her table and was talking to her with gallant deference, but Pibble barely noticed them. He ate slowly and was one of the last to leave the dining room. He found Lady Treadgold waiting in ambush for him.

Lady Treadgold had exercised her talent for inconvenience by insisting on having a sort of counter built for her so that she could eat standing; she had chosen the site for it so as to command the dining room entrance. She lurked there like the Sphinx on the road to Thebes. Either one faced her riddling glare or one got no food.

"Isn't that the most extraordinary coincidence, Mr Pibble?"

"Ur?"

"Surely you haven't forgotten. We were talking about her only the other day—I can't recall why—something to do with geese, killing the geese, Switzerland. No it wasn't Switzerland. Geese, geese . . . how infuriating . . . start somewhere else . . . my husband trained my memory for me, you know. I never used to have one at all . . . it could be quite embarrassing, forgetting which country you were in, Turkey, for instance, at some dinner and getting on

132

to the subject of Armenians and asking the Minister of Justice about those massacres because you'd got it into your head you were in Greece—it was the fisherman's fault, the way they pull on the ropes and sing; you see when I was about nineteen I met this fisherman called Stavros—my dear man, it was an idyll, he couldn't speak English and I couldn't speak Greek—couldn't have been more perfect; when I wanted to bring him home Daddy said he'd have to go into six months' quarantine, which was perfectly ridiculous considering the way Mummy used to smuggle her Cairns in and out . . . that's why I always think I'm in Greece anywhere it's hot enough for the fishermen to strip to the waist . . . Cairns, Daddy, Stavros, Greece, getting poor old Treadgold thrown out of Turkey, training my memory . . . yes, it's like a chain. If you can remember one link you can find the next . . . what was I trying to remember now?"

"Something about geese. You said it was extraordinary."

"It wasn't Greece?"

"Geese."

"I do have my good teeth in, too. Geese, geese . . . start somewhere else . . . this woman, Bunty Jaques—that's it—the *soi-disant* Mr W, tax advantages, geese, Switzerland . . . there! Don't you think that's extraordinary?"

"Are you . . ."

"Of course I am. It's the sort of thing I'm never wrong about. Never! I caught a spy once, you know. I was having luncheon with Nina Phipps at the Café Royal—Nina was having one of her divorces and wanted her hand held and an excuse for a good sob and some oysters; extraordinary woman, used to have cravings just before the case came to court, as if she was pregnant—and there he was. He'd grown a moustache and wasn't wearing his eyeglass and done his hair differently, but I went straight home and rang up Treadgold at his office and said I'd seen this Hun who'd used to be the military attaché in Riga—oh, ten years before, when he was all heel-clicks and the Bolshevik menace—perfectly absurd those young Huns used to be, behaving as though banging their boots together and snatching your hand and kissing it was all that was needed to make you want to leap between the sheets with them, like those birds you see on the television which only have to snap their beaks and blow up their neck-bags to have the females crouching down as though it's the best thing that ever happened to them . . . they hanged him, but they wouldn't let me watch, for some reason . . . yes, I'm right about this woman. She's the one Bunty Jaques picked up, though she's made herself look as different as she can. Not quite sure how to use her stick, you notice?"

"Yes. But she's been ill."

"I think so. I think so. What are you going to do, Mr Pibble?"

"Don't know. Have to . . ."

"Well, don't take too long. You want me to keep my mouth shut, I expect?"

"Please."

"All right, provided *you* do something. Otherwise . . . I'd have made a good detective, wouldn't I?"

She cocked her head into its outrageous-bid position and glared at him, challenging him not to take her seriously. Through his own weariness he was conscious that the challenge was at heart an appeal, a version of the universal appeal of the old, the cry that the world should think of them as something more than feeble and incompetent grotesques.

"Pretty good," he murmured. "Not the paperwork, ur?"

She cackled till she choked, but amid the spasms contrived to wave him away.

Sitting on the lowest stairs, resting for the climb, he became vaguely aware that there was something he was supposed to be doing. It troubled him, because he couldn't connect it either with the unwelcome burden imposed by Lady Treadgold's news (if it was news) or the no more welcome but at least self-imposed task of unravelling Jenny's relationship (if it was a relationship) with Tosca. It didn't even seem to be concerned with the question of

134

whether he could climb the stairs unaided. Or did it? Tottering along the lower passage he had had his doubts, but now, after a surprisingly brief rest, he felt fully up to the effort.

Still he stayed where he was. With returning energy the need to be lying in his own bed, floating in a half-doze, safe from the world, became less urgent. He found himself thinking again about the woman in black. Now, with no struggle, a picture of the Smith trial came back to him. *The slight wait between witnesses. The sense of doubt and frustration after the apparently pliable little landlord of the Plough and Pigeon had proved such a sturdy liar. Shuffling at the side door, usher holding it for the new witness. She stops just inside, outlined for an instant against dark oak, and looks round the court. Her square-shouldered suit is plain but smart, her make-up subdued. She nods to herself, as if accepting the court, accepting the gaze of all those eyes, and only then, as she moved towards the witness box, seems to shrink a little and become frail and timid. "Mary Lou Porter," whispers the Inspector sitting on Pibble's left. "Last time I saw her she was wearing rubies. And not much else." "What were you doing there?" "Guest of Smith's. Typical. Those rubies had never been reported nicked, so he lays on a show to tell us he's got them and we can't do anything about it." "She doesn't look the type." "No."*

She still didn't, supposing it was the same woman. Only the nod woke any positive echo. She was small enough, and slight enough, and must be roughly the right age. The long disassembly line of the years could account for all other modifications to the original model. And the mannerism might have remained. The woman in black had accepted the coffee room with exactly the same gesture as that with which the witness had accepted the court . . . The clothes, too. The combination of smartness and plainness . . . and Mary Lou Isaacs had been in Switzerland, having an operation . . .

Pibble got carefully to his feet and made his way back towards the Incident Room.

Cass was polite, but clearly irritated.

135

"Well, thanks," he said. "I must say I can do without it. The Chief Super's still a bit gone on that side of the case, but . . ." He shrugged.

"He's not here?"

"London."

"Oh."

Well, thought Pibble, that's that. He was turning towards the door when Cass spoke again.

"Don't go for a moment, Mr Pibble. I'd like a word with you. This shot you heard?"

"Uh?"

"Are you still certain about that?"

(Neutral a few seconds before, Cass was now suddenly enemy.)

"As certain as I was in the first place. Fairly but not totally."

"I see . . . You mustn't think I'm getting at you, Mr Pibble. This is a sod of a set-up we've got here. Sometimes I think if I'd had it to myself I'd have sorted it out in twenty-four hours, but the Chief Super . . . I'm not saying anything against him. I can see his problems. He's put almost two years' work in on Wilson, and pushed his luck as far as it would go. I hear along the grapevine that there's one or two up in London who wouldn't mind if he made a mess of it . . . and what it's all been costing the tax-payer! So there's only one way he can look at it, but somehow . . . You know, if he hadn't found *you* down here I don't think he'd be taking quite such a blinkered view of the whole thing. It's as though he's got to prove *you* right, as well as himself."

"I'm sorry, but . . ."

"Forget it. I shouldn't have loosed off at you like that, even if it's still officially my case, which it is, for God's sake! He's only here . . . Oh, forget it! But if you could bring yourself to say something—don't mind what—to let him take a slightly more open-minded . . . Well, I'd be grateful. Sorry. I suppose he'd better know about this other nonsense, if only to show I haven't been dragging my feet. Want me to give him a buzz? Just see if he's in . .

He'll be in touch this evening in any case, and I could pass the old bag's views on then. Hang on . . ."

He dialled, waited, gave an extension number, waited.

"Mike? Busy? Your mate's got a saucy bit of news for you—your side, not mine. I'll pass you over . . ."

Pibble took the handset and started to explain, stammering and urring with the absurdity of the message. Mike listened patiently.

"Well . . . What do you think, Jimmy? Not much by the sound of it."

"Ten minutes ago . . ."

"Of course. Listen, I don't think I can spare a bod who knows her to come and check up. I'm pretty certain she's still in Switzerland. She's on the Move-watch list, but there's a bit of a time-lag there . . . listen, best I can suggest is you take another look at her, talk to her if you get the chance, see what you think then. Now, just supposing Lady T's right—or you even think she might be right—you'd better have a word with our friend. He's got this heart, you know. I don't want him bumping into Mary Lou—or even somebody who looks a bit like Mary Lou—and dropping dead of shock. So he'd better know, either way. Think you can manage that?"

"I expect so."

"Good. You sound a bit brighter, Jimmy."

"I have my ups and downs."

"Keep it up, then. Pass me back to Ted, will you? See you."

Pibble passed the receiver over and rose incautiously enough to bring on the blackness. He came to to find himself still upright propped against the end of the desk, with Cass looking at him with the usual mixture of surprise and pity, tinged with that element of disgust which springs from the knowledge that the watcher will himself one day arrive at this dotage. Pibble scrabbled for his stick and stumped his way out.

Mrs Fowles flapped in the friendly chaos of her office like a hen in a nest-box. ("The shareholders put up with her," Jenny had once said, "because she's a scapegoat. She's untidy for the rest of us.")

"You might have met her, Mr Pibble," piped Mrs Fowles. "Colonel McQueen certainly thought he had. Or said he thought he had," she added shrewdly. "She asked me who you were after we saw you in the coffee room this morning."

"Oh. Did she—"

"It was quite casual, Mr Pibble. She was interested in all the residents, though she'll only be here for a month, I believe. She's convalescing after surgery, you know."

"Is she English?"

"Oh, I think so. Pereira's only her married name. She's led a very interesting life, I should think. She's still rather beautiful, isn't she?"

It had taken Pibble a long time to discover that Mrs Fowles' curious little-girl voice was capable of great subtlety of innuendo. He smiled, and she smiled back.

"I should think you might have met her," she said.

The emphasis of the pronoun was barely perceptible, but enough to imply both that McQueen had not done so and that there was a reason other than pure coincidence why Pibble might.

"Well, thanks," he said. "Do you know if she's been abroad recently?"

"Why, yes. She booked in from—now where's that dratted folder? Bother, I'll have to take that call, Mr Pibble, excuse me . . . hello, Flycatchers . . ."

Pibble mumbled his way out, wondering how much she told enquirers about the other residents—Wilson, for instance.

Again his legs started to totter him towards his room, but he discovered that the notion of dozing now bored him. Keep it up, Mike had said. Keep what up? Never mind . . . voices rose in the bridge room, but when he poked his head round there was only the usual four in action. In the TV room three more residents were watching the dreary routine of week-day racing. The large morning room was empty. It looked like a doze after all. As he passed the coffee room door a waitress started to go back through, pulling the trolley with the urn on it behind her. Holding the door

138

Pibble saw the woman in black sitting, apparently alone, apparently doing nothing, in the chair next to where he'd sat that morning. Deliberately he allowed himself to shrink a little, then doddered in, using his stick more than he needed. He picked up a *Country Life* and lowered himself carefully beside her.

"Hope you don't mind," he muttered. "Usually sit here."

"No."

He read carefully through the gardening article, forcing himself to understand every sentence. When he'd finished he glanced at her. She seemed not to have moved at all, but was staring with trancelike chill attention at a harsh still-life of scarlet poppies on the wall above the side-board. It made him feel painfully absurd and dotardly, trying to break in on this striking stranger.

"Wilt," he mumbled. "Fellow says he's got the answer."

"Oh."

"I wonder if he's right. I wish I'd known that twenty years ago."

"Twenty years you've had it?"

"Me? Oh, no. At least . . . It's a clematis disease."

"Oh."

Silence gripped the room like a closed fist. Pibble was about to return to his magazine when she moved, very slightly but enough to break the trance.

"Clemaytis, you mean?" she said. "I never had room for clemaytis, nor the depth of soil, neither. Only had the roof, you see? I used to grow some fancy begonias up there when I was a kid."

Her voice was still light and slow, but a sudden warmth had come into it, together with a distinct East London twang. The contrast with her formidably *haut bourgeois* mask was sharp and pleasing.

"Did you?" said Pibble. "So did I, for three or four years, until my wife made me pack them in."

"Why would she want to do that?"

"Some fool suggested they were vulgar, so we started a grey border instead. Artemisias and things. At least they were less trouble than begonias."

"Real sods, begonias can be," she said. "Myself, I prefer a bit of vulgarity."

She looked directly at him as if for agreement. Her eyes seemed preternaturally dark, contrasted with the nacreous skin of illness.

"I suppose you can do what you like on a roof," he said. "In the front garden, you've got the neighbours to think of."

"Oh, we had the customers up on the roof, summer. My Dad kept this pub, see?"

"Was that the Blue Bear?"

Without a muscle moving her face became that of another woman. The dark eyes were wet pebbles, the cheekbones declared the skull, the mouth was a predator's. At once he had no doubt who he was talking to, though this persona was further than ever from the shaken little witness of thirty years ago. He thought that she was going to deny the connection, but evidently she felt herself too imperious for that level of lying.

"I heard as you'd retired," she said. "You want to keep your nose clean now, mister. They haven't the same interest in seeing you're looked after."

"I'm sorry," he muttered. "I didn't mean . . ."

She watched him, half fury, half contempt.

"I *have* retired, of course," he said. "I'm not very interested in anything that happens now. I don't know what's going on. But . . . do you remember the Smith trial?"

Again her face changed, warier now, but interested.

"Suppose I do?"

"There was a defence witness, a Miss Potter?"

She nodded, that characteristic flick of the head, accepting the safer formality of the third person.

"She broke down under cross-examination, and the defence fell to pieces as a result. I'd like to know if she went to bits on purpose."

"Why?"

"The Smith case—it made a lot of difference to me. I suppose you could say it changed my life."

She turned away and leaned back a little, gazing at the blood-coloured poppies.

"Mary Lou Potter," she said, almost dreamily. "What we used to call a good-time girl, that's all she was. Vernon Smith's tart, and he thought he owned her. He thought he owned her, like he owned his hat and his shoes and his motor car. If he wanted her to swan about stark naked, part from a load of rubies, in front of his friends, then that's what she did. I suppose . . . d'you know that hymn, mister? Once to every man and nation comes the moment to decide? I suppose she decided it wasn't going to happen no more. From now on she was going to be somebody else, not a good-time girl, not anybody's tart, ever again. Yes, that's when it happened. You aren't the only one what it made a bit of difference to, mister."

"No, I expect not. Did you ever meet Richard Foyle?"

She laughed. "Dickie Foyle! Now he was a case!"

"What do you mean?"

"Thought such a lot of himself."

"So did the Smiths, I imagine."

"Course—but that's different. Listen, I known a lot of big men since those days or ones what thought they was big. The Smiths, they was quite a common type—they knew right from wrong, fair enough, but they didn't care. It was just rules, what they'd always got away with breaking, see? Then there's the ones what honestly don't know, they don't grasp as there's rules at all, if you follow me. That sort never get very far, cause of not understanding what makes anyone else tick. They can be quite brainy, but they're thick with it. Morally thick, if you follow. And then there's Dickie Foyle's sort—they know right from wrong, too; but it doesn't apply to them, because they're God. They're above it. I expect Hitler was that sort."

"Very likely."

"I tell you something might interest you. Dickie Foyle, he bowled that Potter girl over first time she met him. When you're running around with a bunch of yobbos, meeting a bloke as can actually talk, one as seems interested in what *you* think, too . . ."

141

"Yes, he was very good at that."

"Well, couple of times when Vernon was busy, she went off with Dickie. They went to Malta, once, and once just down to Kent, had a good time. Then there was that business about stripping off in front of all those fellows and wearing them rubies, and after that she had a bit of a row with Vernon and she went and let him know as she and Dickie had been having good times together. Vernon, I said as he thought he owned her. All he did at the time was rough her up a little, but he took it into his head he was going to fix Dickie. Can you guess what he did?"

"He tortured and murdered a man called Duggie Canino?" She didn't seem at all surprised.

"That's right. He was killing two birds with one stone, see? He was frightening off the Mafia, same time, but the idea was he'd get Dickie to have the body found—something to do with a car with blood in it which Dickie could say he'd worked out—only *then* it would turn out as Dickie couldn't of worked it out that way, length of time they took killing Duggie. Vernon said it was about time somebody noticed about Dickie, so he wasn't going to be much use no longer. He decided to give that somebody something to notice."

The drizzle, the creaking capes, the scarlet-patterned limb.

"That was me," said Pibble. "I think he may have been a bit suspicious. He worked it so that I found Canino, and he wouldn't admit it had been his idea to search that bit of waste. He said he wanted me to have the credit."

"Yes," she said. "The Potter girl tipped him to watch out. She didn't want him to go down, particular—it was Vernon what she was after. She'd been giving Dickie bits about Vernon; you see, Vernon had got Dickie wrong. Vernon couldn't understand that Dickie wasn't through-and-through bent. Spite of everything, Dickie always saw hisself as a thief-taker, and all along he'd been fixing to get the Smiths when it suited him, piling the evidence away. She was sorry when he went down, but there wasn't anything she could do about it—she had to look after herself, see?

142

She couldn't let Vernon guess as she had anything to do with what Dickie'd got hold of . . . and Dickie played fair about that, didn't he? Never let on?"

"No. I never realised . . ."

"Course, I can't say it was all for the Potter girl's sake. He'd be trying to get as much credit as he could for hisself, if he was going to get them to let him turn Queen's evidence . . . only they wasn't wearing that."

"King's evidence," murmured Pibble.

"King's? Long ago as that? I suppose so. Sometimes it seems like yesterday."

"Yes . . . Did you know Duggie Canino?"

"Never met him. What you thinking? My . . . the Potter girl's first boy-friend? Too neat that would of been, don't you think? Tell you what, though, Vernon picked him cause of the way he'd once seen him smiling."

"I thought it was because he was working with the Mafia."

"Oh yes, there was that," she said, almost dismissively, as though the irritation of a grimace weighed heavier. Silence fell again, but companionable now, almost like the accepted non-communications of marriage. Pibble began to gather his energies for rising from the chair and leaving. He would have liked to tell her that he would have to pass on to Mike that she was there, but to do so would be to acknowledge that Mike wanted to know, and that in turn would prove that Wilson was at Flycatchers.

"You got any regrets?" she said in wholly conversational tones, as though raising the subject of the weather.

"I suppose so," said Pibble. "I expect most people have, really, whatever they say."

"Pillars of salt," she said. "No, that ain't what I meant. I was only talking about Vernon. And Dickie. Before you come in, even . . . Funny, perhaps it was seeing you here before and knowing who you was . . . I was sitting looking at them poppies and thinking as I'd never liked red anyway. I wonder, if it had been sapphires instead of rubies . . . No, I suppose not . . ."

143

"Were those the Ilford rubies?" asked Pibble.

Her eyes widened slightly.

"That's right," she said. "How did you know? I thought they wasn't never on file, cause of supposing to have got lost in a yachting accident."

"Something somebody told me."

"It's a funny world that," she said. "Nobs, I'm talking about. Few years back I got interested in them. I suppose I thought as I'd like to meet a different class of people from what I'm used to. But in some ways it was just the same—nobody ever saying anything out straight, for instance. And gangs. And there being things, like them rubies, what everyone knew what had really happened, only they wasn't letting on . . . You know, when Vernon got hold of something like that he wouldn't use a fence if he could help it. Always tried to sell it direct back to the owner. That's what he did when he got hold of them rubies . . . had a bent lawyer what did the tricky business. I can tell you Vernon wasn't half put out when this feller reports back with his Lordship's compliments, saying his Lordship had only laughed and said to tell him as he'd done him a service . . . Do you know, I think it was cause of that as Vernon laid on that party where the Potter girl wore the rubies. He could never stand being laughed at, Vernon, so all he could think of was to pass the insult on, get the laugh on someone else. He thought he'd rile the cops a bit, letting 'em see he had them rubies and they couldn't touch him cause of their not being stolen property, see? So he threw this party and invited the cops along . . . You wasn't one of them, by any chance?"

"No."

"Glad to hear it," she said, with a very faint twitch of the thin lips. "It ain't the sort of introduction . . . talking of nobs, ain't you a bit of a fish out of water in a place like this?"

"A friend's paying for me—a very rich man. I worked for him after I retired."

"How long've you been here?"

"Six or seven months."

"Heard anything?"

"What sort of . . ."

"Our sort of thing. Something dicey about Flycatchers."

"Drugs?"

"Might be . . . only that don't smell right. Tell you, I was having coffee with one of my nobby friends—charity committee we called it, but it wasn't really more than a hen-party with mink and pearls—and this place came up in the talk. It was just the way one of them said it and another of them twitched, and I thought *hello, there's something dicey there.* You get a nose, don't you?"

Pibble shook his head. Was she fishing for news of Wilson? If so it was a very oblique cast, but the possibility made him nervous. He tried to strike a closing note, so that he could leave without seeming to be going anywhere in particular.

"I think we'd have got the Smiths anyway," he said. "As you say, Dickie was building up to it, and if he hadn't tripped up too I think he'd have managed things much more cleanly than we did without him. But as it was . . . No, I don't regret that it happened, but I regret very much that it was me who caused it to happen."

She nodded, accepting the banality, and returned to the vision of redness in the poppies. To her it was rubies, but to Pibble it was blood, and he wanted no knowledge of it. The momentum of going re-built itself. He laid the magazine down, gripped his stick and the arm of the chair and carefully drew himself forward and up. The blackness hovered, murmured, but never quite enclosed him. He was already moving towards the door when she spoke again.

"You know," she said dreamily. "I think if things had turned out a bit different I might of married Dickie Foyle. What become of him anyway?"

"He got full remission, of course. He went out to Australia. Died about a year ago."

"I wish I'd known," she said. "And did he make a go of it out there?"

"I'm told he died a millionaire."

"You see?" she said.

Nine

IT WAS STRANGE to stand at his own door, peer through the one-way glass and see his own bed empty, made and waiting with the cover turned enticingly back; and Jenny, too, sitting in her usual chair, reading. It all gave Pibble a sense of being risen from the tomb to a more spiritual plane of life, except that his body was still agreeably with him, having climbed the stairs without exhaustion, and being now far from enticed by the bed. Jenny broke her marble, mourning-angel stillness by turning a page. The movement was absurdly reassuring; it seemed much too simple and natural for anybody with a load of worry, let alone guilt, on her mind.

Pibble let himself stand for a good minute, simply watching. When she turned another page he moved quietly on.

Wilson's room lay beyond the fire-doors, down a short side-passage. As Pibble turned the last corner he found himself face to face with a young man in a dark jacket and jeans. He had his hand in his jacket pocket and inspected Pibble with a combination of caution and boredom, a look which Pibble knew well.

"I'm James Pibble. I'm a patient here, but I know Chief Superintendent Crewe. He asked me to bring a message to Mr Wilson."

The sentry studied him for a moment in silence, then nodded.

"Nurse was along, asking had I seen you," he said, speaking in a near-mutter and half out of the side of his mouth, as though

146

somehow the medical conspiracy were as great a danger as the criminal one.

"I'll be about five minutes," said Pibble.

The man nodded and stood aside.

Wilson was watching the racing. He slouched in his chair, his whole pose sullenly rejecting the factitious thrill of the commentary. The dull eyes glanced at Pibble and returned to the screen. Three horses rose in apparent slow motion to a fence. One fell over. The other two galloped across muddy turf. Jockeys belaboured rumps. The front horse didn't seem to be moving very fast, but the camera followed it so that the second horse galloped backwards, out of the screen. A grandstand floated by, with about twenty spectators sprinkled along it. Most of them had umbrellas up. The winning-post slid unemphatically past. The losing horse, now about twenty yards behind, slowed to a walk before it reached it. There seemed to be no more runners. Wilson pressed a gadget in his hand and though the picture remained the voices died.

"Cat's meat," he said. "They get it back out of the cans and reconstitute it into horses, and then they call it racing. Ever strike you as everything as seems to make life better makes it worse?"

"Ur?"

"Take racing. Forty years back, standing out there in the sodding rain, what wouldn't I have given to be able to watch it all in the warm, in my own room? Now that's what I'm doing, and you know what? It's not hardly racing. They got to put something on, but where's the horses? Why, they're fetching them back out of the knackers to give the cameras something to look at. Lucky for you you're not a racing man."

"No. But I remember stand-up comics."

"Right. Living a whole year on just three routines, you mean? Not that I bothered with them much—it's not something villains go in for, I suppose. Funny, I hadn't thought of that before. Course, there were jokers, but a laugh just for the sake of a laugh . . . You got something to tell me then?"

147

"What? Oh, er, yes . . . Mike Crewe asked me to have a word with you."

"Serious, is it?"

"Possibly. Just a question of warning you so that it didn't get sprung on you unawares."

"Fire away. I won't drop dead, I promise."

"It's about Mrs Isaacs."

"Ah."

"I've been talking to her."

"Phone?"

"No, in the coffee room."

"You don't say."

Wilson sounded completely unperturbed, more interested in the horse steaming in the winner's enclosure than in what Pibble was saying.

"I think what happened is this," said Pibble. "She's been in Switzerland having an operation, but things started to get out of hand at the Blue Bear, so she came home before she'd finished convalescing to try and sort things out. My impression is that her friends told her you were here, but that her organisation had got a bit chaotic while she was away, and she didn't believe them. She needed to be in a nursing home anyway, so she decided to come down here and see for herself."

"She say whether they killed George?"

"No. I couldn't ask . . . it'd have been admitting the connection between this place and the Blue Bear . . ."

"Suppose you're right. How is the old bag, anyway?"

"Frail. She had that pearly look. She seemed a bit fed up."

"Mary Lou!"

For the first time Wilson sounded surprised, even faintly alarmed.

"She was in a what's-it-all-for-anyway mood," said Pibble.

"I don't believe it. She didn't scare the pants off you, then?"

"No. She looked pretty formidable, but she talked in a rather cosy way about begonias and things."

"What things?"

"The Smith case, mostly. She told me Vernon Smith deliberately saw to it that Richard Foyle got spotted. By me, as it happened. Then she arranged things so that Smith himself got entangled in his own net. Apparently it was because Smith had made her walk about in front of his friends wearing nothing except some rubies."

"You don't say! You don't say! I remember hearing about that—knew a feller what was there. I don't suppose . . ."

He was looking at the ceiling now, sounding as wistful as a child.

"I'd give a lot to have a word with her," he said.

"I doubt if the Chief Superintendent . . ."

"And why not? Mary Lou'd remember a pile of things what I've forgot. This sort of case, anyway, the more witnesses you get . . . I'll have trouble making anyone believe me, all by myself, won't I? But if Mary Lou's in that kind of mood, and we could persuade her . . . You're missing something, you know, only seeing her like this. When she's her proper self she can strike sparks off of a lump of cream cheese."

"Well," said Pibble. "I suppose I could suggest . . ."

Wilson interrupted him by a sudden movement of the hand, slight but imperiously effective. Pibble, who had been standing all this while propped on his stick, turned to see the door opening. For a moment he expected to see Mrs Isaacs stalk into the room, her proper self, lethal with sparks, but in fact it was only Maisie bringing round the afternoon post—another invariable item in the Flycatchers' routine. She had a smallish parcel with the letters.

"Hello, beautiful," said Wilson. "Brought something for your uncle, then?"

Maisie produced her strange, vague smile and gave him the parcel.

"It's been through the metal detector," she said, as though the words had no meaning to her at all. Pibble guessed that her whole attention was far away, galloping with Lord Hawkside along the cliff road while the lightning flashed and the smuggler-swarming sea rolled its waves in thunder to the beaches.

"Has it now? That's good. Spot of class there, Pibble, don't you think? They didn't have to install the doofer special for me, cause they'd got one already, case of someone having a go at some of the wogs you get holidaying here. Bring us a knife, miss, so as I can open it. Ta. Now give your uncle a kiss. Ta. And now you can go."

Still in her dream, Maisie performed her tasks like an automaton. She gave the impression that if Wilson had told her to do a belly dance or to jump out of the window she would have done so with the same dazed grace. Wilson licked his upper lip as he watched her go.

"What couldn't I have done with a few of that model, forty years back," he said. "Doesn't know if she's in this world or the next, does she?"

As if reminded by the movement of his tongue he took his roll of peppermints out of his pocket and inspected it, then put it back. His other hand caressed the parcel.

"You still bent, mate?" he said suddenly. "Like we fixed?"

"Ur."

Pibble's mutter of assent came from only a pocket of his mind. *Doesn't know if she's in this world or the next, does she? . . . I don't think she ever realised what was happening to her. I hope not . . . So do I.* The image of the Balham poisoner swam into focus. Maisie's replaced it. Lord Hawkside whipped his foundering mare along the cliff road. Tosca lay face up in the snow-storm, dead romantic. Maisie. *I was washing Jenny's hair.* The shock of revelation faded to the wearisomeness of having to re-think all his thoughts.

"You know what this is, don't you?" said Wilson.

There was a throb of ecstasy in his voice. His hand trembled slightly as he sliced the Sellotape exactly down the line where the brown paper joined. The process looked much the same as that with which he unwrapped his peppermints, but its drive was clearly different, not an exercise in power, but a heightening of lust by anticipation. He was like a lover stripping his mistress with

150

luxurious ritual to nakedness.

"Ur," said Pibble, welcoming the summons back into the here and now.

The parcel was square-edged, about nine inches by four by two. A white sticker-label addressed it to Wilson at Flycatchers. It had been sealed with a practised precision that suggested an old-fashioned shop. Pibble was not sure whether he could already smell the tobacco, and the fainter odour of the cedar-wood box, or whether that was auto-suggestion.

"Slipped through, I suppose," said Wilson. "George used to stop the postman and take them off of him, only he missed a couple of times . . . thought it was going to be like that from now on . . . Got a new feller doing them up, by the look of it . . . ah . . ."

He laid the box in its wax-paper inner wrapping to one side, took a gold lighter from his dressing-gown pocket and lit the brown paper at one corner, holding it expertly so that the flame burnt across it in an even march, blue at the leading edge and yellow, almost white, where the picrid smoke trailed upward from the rim. Black flakes wavered to the carpet. Wilson ignored them, as if used to spoiling expensive furnishing, relishing the destruction, even. Power again.

"Always burn the evidence, my granny told me," he purred.

When the final corner was almost scorching his fingers he let it fall, still flaming, to a point where he could shuffle his slippered heel on to it, then turned to the box again, raising the seal of the wax-paper with his knife and folding it back. He slit the seal of the box itself, laid his knife down, cradled the box between his two palms and eased its lid up with his thumbs. For several seconds he stared at the ranked contents.

"That ain't right," he said.

He picked out one of the cigars and rolled it between thumb and forefinger.

"What the . . ."

With a violent movement he rammed the cigar back, then peered at the whole box.

"The bitch!" he shouted. "The sodding . . ."

He flung the box into the corner of the room. A heave, a spasm, and he was standing, turning to face Pibble. His lips were purple, his cheeks yellow and scarlet. He stood there, his mouth dragging down and sideways in wrenched jerks. His right hand rose, griped like a bird's foot at his chest, twice. He fell. There was the slow thump of his falling and then he was lying face down, still except that his hand continued to gripe· at the carpet and his breath gargled painfully in this throat.

Pibble almost fell himself, getting his stick tangled in his legs as he scurried to the door. He heaved it open.

"Heart-attack!" he gasped.

The sentry sprang from his half-lounge against the wall, drew a pistol from his pocket and rushed past Pibble into the room, holding the gun in the position he had been taught, as though he hoped to tame the rebellious organ by threatening to shoot it. At a flapping shuffle which was almost a run Pibble went to fetch Jenny.

"Sorry about that," said Mike. "You can't really blame Shanklin."

"Course not."

Pibble lay with his eyes half-closed, feeling that all the bright essences had been drained from him, leaving him a papery shell which needed the bedclothes to hold it from crumbling into mummy-dust.

"Makes a change, getting arrested yourself . . . What's up? Jimmy!"

"All right. Only . . . last thing Dickie said to me."

The rictus-smile, the jaunty nod, the almost insane sparkle in the eye-balls.

"Foyle? Rum how he keeps cropping up, isn't it?"

"I'm sorry."

"Don't apologise, Jimmy. I know how you feel—at least I half-know. There are one or two people in everybody's life, I expect . . .

Totems, if you see that I mean. As a matter of fact, you're one of mine."

"Uh!"

"That's right. I've never really thought about it till now, but I suppose I've always tended to use you as a sort of standard . . . and suppose when we were working together I'd discovered you weren't the totally straight copper I'd taken you for . . ."

"Mike!"

"All right. Take it easy. I didn't mean to embarrass you. Let's change the subject . . . Where were we . . . Shanklin . . ."

"Did the right thing," Pibble managed to mutter.

"Glad you think so. He says that nurse of yours asked him to handcuff you to the bed."

"Wilson?"

"Dead. On his way to the surgery. Took eighteen months' hard work with him, not to mention the tax-payer's money this place cost us. Joke cigars! The sort that blow up in your face! Jesus! Who'd have imagined . . ."

"But the box . . ."

"Oh, that was pukka—we've talked to the shop. Wilson had left an order with them and they'd been sending him a box once a week. The people here intercepted the first two or three, and told him they'd done so on medical grounds, and after that they stopped coming. We assumed he'd cancelled the order, and the shop assumed he was getting them, and as he'd paid for a year's supply in advance they went on sending them. Somebody must have been nicking them somewhere in the pipeline and having a regular luxury smoke."

"No. Tosca. Intercepted parcel. Took Wilson for drives. Smoked in car."

"It makes me sick! So that's how she knew what brand of box—Tosca'd told her. All she'd got to do was buy the right cigars, plus enough of the joke ones, take the seals off carefully, transfer the bands, seal the whole thing up and send it off. Yes, and she'd know they were being intercepted, too, so she came down to see if she

153

couldn't get round the system. Mrs Fowles, who's not as scatty as she looks, by any means, had actually spotted it and put it aside, but somebody must have nipped in and put it back with the mail for distribution. Jesus, she's got a nerve. But she's gone too far this time."

"Not Mary Lou."

"What do you mean?"

"Talking to her. Just before. Not her idea."

"Sure?"

"No . . . Listen. Wilson. Wanted you to get her to turn Queen's Evidence."

Through the daze of weariness he saw Mike's face change as the glare of simple rejection knotted itself to a frown. Pibble fumbled up another scraping of energy.

"Think she might," he whispered. "Power over men. Ever since Vernon Smith. Always been her drive. Told me."

"You don't say! Jimmy, you must have made a hit with her, and far as I know she's never fancied anybody except a line of rather bum black boxers before. I wonder if you're right . . . The Blue Bear lot are a handful at any time, and if she's been as ill as she looks . . . I wouldn't have known her, honest. Which reminds me, that old gas-bag of yours . . ."

"Ur?"

"It's all a bit iffy . . . Ted Cass—he's good, going to be very good—but he hasn't liked having me around with my line on the case. Tell you the truth, there was quite a bit of resentment because we'd never told them down here what we were up to at Flycatchers. He really didn't want to know anything about my side . . . But now Mary Lou's turned up, he's rather got to . . . except he's found an out. In fact he's taking the line that if your friend Lady Treadgold is as on the spot as all that, then she might be right about the other guff she's been feeding you. He'll have to tread bloody careful, won't he?"

"Ur. Talked to Maisie?"

"Who? Oh, that crazy nurse. Nothing there. She picked up the

154

post as usual and took it round. The parcel was with the rest of it, except that Mrs Fowles says it wasn't. Answer, Mary Lou. What makes you think it wasn't her, Jimmy? Admittedly it's not her style—much more like her to send a hit man round—but she might try it as a once off. Not a bad idea—bloke with a dicey heart having a relaxing smoke, and the thing blows up in his face. It really might make him drop dead, and even if it didn't it'd very likely scare him out of giving us the help we want. Uh?"

"She'd know about cigars. Know he'd spot it. Never get as far as lighting one. Couldn't know he'd . . . Anger more than shock, anyway."

"Um."

"She didn't say anything else?"

"She's not even telling us the time till she's got her lawyers standing round her . . . still, you could be half right; one of her lads might have set the thing up without telling her, and when she got back she decided she'd better come down and see if she could make it all work. Show them she's still in charge, spite of having half her guts missing. What d'you think of that, Jimmy?"

"Ur."

The mist of weariness closed in, blanking all perceptions. Before it became impenetrable the shapes of the landscape loomed and changed. *She didn't say anything else?* Old fool, how do you expect them to listen to your mumbles? They'll go on talking about what they want to talk about, as if you'd never tried to show them, tell them . . .

"Bye now, Jimmy. Sorry if I've worn you out. You've been a great help."

"Ur."

He woke from fathomless sleep and knew at once that Jenny was in the room. The awareness was enough to prevent him dolphining back at once beneath the surface, but even so it seemed an effort (very like that of a swimmer dragging his body into the weightfulness of air) to force himself fully awake. He spoke with

155

closed eyes.

"Jenny?"

"You old monster! Sleuthing around, giving my patients heart-attacks, getting yourself arrested!"

Her voice, low with conspiracy and chuckling faintly with the fun of it, came from somewhere near the window. Wilson's death seemed not to have perturbed her at all. Was it that Flycatchers was a place of death, and she was calloused against it? Or that her energies were all so natural that she simply accepted death as natural too? Or . . .

"Sorry," he whispered. "Want you to help me. Got to talk to Maisie."

A long pause.

"Why?" she said, wary now.

"Got to stop all this."

"All what?"

"Murders."

Another pause.

"I don't think it'll do any good, Jimmy. You're a clever old thing, but honestly I don't think you'll get anywhere. I've tried to ask her a couple of times, but she goes into a sort of trance. All she can say is she was helping me wash my hair."

"She wasn't."

"No. But that's what she remembers. She only gets normal again if I talk as if I remembered it too."

"Normal?"

"She's perfectly normal—most of the time."

"Always been like that?"

"No. I mean, she's had these sort of fits—they're a bit like epilepsy with the physical symptoms left out—oh, for a year or two now. About once a fortnight, I suppose. Usually I just yell at her, or slap her face, and she blinks and doesn't remember anything. Only, since that night . . ."

"Ur."

"But listen, Jimmy. This other thing—Mr X—that's nothing to

do with her. She was just taking the post round. She always does."

"No."

"What do you mean? You aren't suggesting Maisie went out and bought a box of best cigars and . . ."

"No."

"And joke cigars, too. Do you know what that reminds me of?"

"Foster-Banks."

"Oh, you're impossible! Do you always know what people are thinking? In that case why aren't you better at bridge? Lady Treadgold says you . . . no, that's not fair."

"I want to talk to her."

He heard her footsteps whisper across the carpet. He opened his eyes and saw her leaning above him, very serious.

"Listen," she said. "If you shop Maisie, then that's the end. You understand."

"Yes."

"You understand I actually mean it? It'll make me think different about you?"

"Yes."

"But you'd still do it?"

"Don't know till I've talked to her."

"You would, though. You know, I believe you'd shop me if you thought I killed George."

"Did for a bit."

She stared at him, astounded. The possibility had evidently never entered her mind. He watched her beginning to think it out, tracing his footsteps through the maze, so he was ready for the sudden ugly flush that mottled her clear skin, and the look of appalled hurt and anger which meant that she was confronting the phallic herm in the cul-de-sac of dark yew.

"Knew it was impossible," he said, deliberately clear but leaving the *it* unspecified.

"Am I mad, Jimmy?" she whispered.

"No. Crippen no."

"Only I sometimes think . . . everybody else . . ."

157

"Not everybody."

"It's all right if you're queer," she said. "It's all right if you sleep around. It's all right, even, sort of, if you molest kids—I mean they'll try to stop you, of course, but somehow . . . the only thing that isn't right is not wanting any of it, not wanting to talk about it or think about it, even. That's what's unnatural."

"Stupid word."

"What do you mean?"

"Too many different meanings. My dear, nothing you do, or don't do, is unnatural."

He hadn't intended the emphasis on the pronoun, had meant it to be a mere generality, but the phrase came out as particular to her.

"My last job," she said. "I thought I was enjoying it. I shared a room with a girl called Penny. I was going off duty one morning and I was passing one of the linen cupboards and I heard a noise, so I opened the door. It was Penny and one of the porters. He'd got his trousers round his ankles. She . . . When the door opened, they sort of froze and then they saw who it was and laughed and went on. I don't think they'd have minded if I'd stayed and watched them."

"That's why you came here?"

"Sort of. I tried to explain to Penny later. I wanted to change my room, you see. I wanted her to understand that I liked her, but . . . And the porter—they weren't in love or anything, it was just like having a cup of coffee with someone—he started grinning at me. And he told some of the other men, and they . . . *I* was the freak, you see. I am a freak, aren't I?"

"No."

She spread her short-fingered hands above the bed, showing him them.

"I was never finished. Look. I'm a Friday car."

"Ur?"

"The ones the workmen leave bits out of because they want to knock off for the weekend. That's me. I've never shown you my

158

feet, have I? They're ridiculous."

"You told me about your shoes. Don't worry, my dear. I think there are quite a lot of us about—afraid to touch, don't like to be touched."

"Us?"

"Yes. And we usually find each other, I think."

"Lady Treadgold says you're going to marry me."

"Ur. Not sure about that. Too convenient? You nurse me, I shield you . . ."

"Oh, Jimmy, there's more to it than that!"

"You think so?"

"Yes, I really do!"

"Um. I'd like to think so . . . But there is that too, uh?"

"I suppose so . . . Well?"

"Later. Feet. What size are Maisie's?"

"I don't want to talk about Maisie's feet. I want to talk about whether we're going to get married."

"Please."

"Fives, very slim, and they make me green with envy. Now . . ."

"Shoes wet?"

"What do you mean?"

"When she came in."

"Yes, soaked. Now, about . . ."

"Carrying the pistol?"

"How did you know? I was in her room, using her drier. I always do because she's got a lot of fancy kit for her own hair, and I help her with that, you see. She came through the door like a ghost and stood there, holding this gun as if she had no idea what it was. I was amazed when I saw it wasn't a toy. I asked her where she'd got it, and she said there'd been a duel on the castle roof. I couldn't think what she was talking about, but I was frightened, so I told her to give me the gun. Do you know, she curtseyed? But she gave it to me, and a key as well, and just stood there. I took her cloak off her, and that was frightening too. She began smiling, but she went very pale and trembled at the same time. I put her cloak

159

on and ran down to the staff door, because I thought it must be that key, and it was. My first idea was to throw the gun into the bushes somewhere, but when I got out I heard the tower door slamming in the wind, and I thought that might be what she meant by the castle, so I went and had a look. I went right up the stairs. The roof was open too, and I found him there."

"Dead?"

"Yes. I turned him over to check. Then I stopped and thought for a bit. There were some gloves in the pocket of the cloak, so I put them on, and I wiped the gun on the cloak and tucked it in under the body on the far side. I bolted the roof door when I went out, but I couldn't find the key to the bottom door. I thought the longer it was before anybody found the body the harder it'd be to pin it on Maisie. Do you know, when I got back, she was standing just where I'd left her, still smiling in that funny actressy way, just as if I hadn't been gone any time at all. I had to slap her face to wake her up. She couldn't remember anything. I told her she'd been helping me wash my hair, and her shoes were wet because she'd spilt some of the water over them. I told her to take them down to the drying room, and her cloak—there'd be plenty of others there, because it had been raining or snowing all day—and then I came rushing along to look after you because I knew you timed all my movements. I had to skip my poor old veg to be on time."

"I see."

"But listen, Jimmy. I'm not going to have you shopping Maisie, not at any price. You understand that? Not at any price."

"Um . . . Try not to . . . tell me—don't be angry—important . . . this other girl you knew—Penny—Maisie like that?"

"No! No, of course not!"

"Not at all? She looks . . ."

"Yes, she does, but . . . blokes are always having a go at her, naturally, and I expect sometimes . . . we don't talk about it, but I expect she's sometimes . . . I mean, if it's the right bloke she probably enjoys it in a vague sort of way. I don't know. Really, I

160

think the only people she's ever been properly in love with are the heroes in her toshy books."

"Tosca."

"No! Honestly not, Jimmy. He'd tried before, about six weeks ago. She was very upset. I'm quite sure about that, because she's really used to it—men trying to get off with her, I mean—and usually it doesn't bother her. But this time she seemed to be having one of her fits. She was very muddled. I couldn't make out who she was talking about for a bit. I thought it was old Follicle who'd had a go at her. She adores him, of course, but not like that—more as if he were her father—but then I worked out who she meant. Really, Jimmy, she wouldn't touch Tosca with a barge-pole!"

"Those clothes. Douglas Fairbanks. Hero in her book."

"Oh! And the way she curtseyed to me! And that smile when I took her cloak off! Listen, Jimmy, I've just thought of something else. This morning, when we were looking at the tower and talking about cloaks catching in the roses . . ."

"Bat's wing . . ."

"That's right. When I was undoing the cloak she said something in a funny voice, like a man's. I can't remember the exact words, but it was about looking like a bat's wing from above . . . You mean, George Tosca found out—or thought he'd found out—what she really liked, and tried to lay it on for her, but he got it wrong. He wasn't the hero, he was the villain, and she was the heroine and she shot him with his own gun!"

"No."

Pibble's eyelids dragged themselves down across his eyes; no power on earth could have heaved them open. But the Old Guard was still marching, still trailing its leaden pikes, though rank after rank slept as they trudged. He felt his lips move, whispering his last thought as he gave himself to darkness.

"The shoes don't fit."

Ten

"Ah, Major Pibble."

"Sir."

"You were a policeman, I see."

"Sir."

"How have you spent your war?"

"Enemy aliens, to begin with, sir. Then mostly liaison with Civilian Police and Department J."

"Yes, yes."

The unknown Colonel, a small, fungussy man, his voice weary with decisions, glanced through Pibble's file. Dismal little underground office. Illumination designed for headaches. Nine telephones on desk.

"Going back to the force, Major?"

"Sir."

"Well, we've got you for a month, and I've got a that-sized job. Semi-sensitive. General done himself in. Rooms in Albany. Straight suicide, your civvy colleagues say—his batman had left him . . ."

The dead voice softened to a note of query, expecting a response.

"Homo, sir?"

"Right. One of a cosy little club. Household names, some of them. Our problem is, this fellow was writing his memoirs. Made an ass of himself somewhere in Italy, due to be bowler-hatted, only his pansy friends got him posted to a cushy job in London District, plenty of time to do a bit of writing, uh?"

162

"You want me to go through the papers, sir."

"Good man. It's a two-edged problem, Pibble. First, is there anything in there which would get anyone who counts into a mess? You'll be surprised who some of them are. We may have to take protective action. Second, and this really matters rather more, who are the others? I don't know whether you realise it, but the war's nothing like as over as we think it is, and these people are security risks . . ."

Why? Why now? What unnoticed scuffling among the memory-banks had brought this forgotten episode to the surface as he lay half-dozing in the artificial dusk of his room? All practical logic demanded that he should have been adding what Jenny had told him to the near-completed jigsaw, all emotional logic that he should have been weighing the enticingness of marriage to Jenny against the absurdity and disgust of such a union. Instead he was sitting in a tall room, in that backwater above Piccadilly. *Soft maroon leather on the chairs, two Corots and a Fragonard, apparently genuine, a curious faint odour like the remains of incense. And he was glancing through an apparently endless pile of letters exchanged with a female second cousin about the precise names of childhood ponies and servants and the dates of Scottish holidays. There was even a map of the secret pathways among the laurels around a Yorkshire mansion. All the other boxes contained similar letters, to and from many other correspondents. Not one of them referred to a date later than the General's tenth birthday. It was as though his life had stopped there.*

Why now? The wish to know became urgent. Irritably he flogged the dead donkey of his mind. Lady Treadgold's system, then . . . laurel-map, the papers, the General, the Queers' Club, sexual aberrations, Jenny? Tchah! Nothing like it. The laurel-map, the papers, the fungussy Colonel, the last posting before demob, the sense of change impending, Jenny again? No. The laurel-map, the papers, the smell in the room, incense, burning paper, burning the evidence, Wilson? No . . .

At last he gave up by making the conscious decision to attempt

163

to think about something else. Jenny. Am I mad? The episode in the linen-cupboard, central but strangely banal. *Us*, Pibble had said, but it wasn't quite honest. He was (had been) merely timid all his life, not horrified—and even so was conscious of a distant kinship with other souls whose timidity took more extreme forms . . .

Cadogan Square, the ponderous respectability of that unweatherable brick. Sir Somebody's daughter missing from first-floor flat. (Harrods decor: Regency stripe on the walls, buff-coloured tassle fringes on the lampshades.) Sir Somebody's nephew, tenant of attic flat in same house, six and a half feet tall, gawky as a mantis, flop of black hair; routine questions, nudge of doubt, search. Girl on bed, not dead but almost, encased in home-made armour, with hinged flaps through which a timid finger could explore, and that was all. No charges. "They'll probably marry," Dickie Foyle had said.

Foyle! "Rum how he keeps cropping up, isn't it?" Mike. Totems. That was the connection—obsessions—the pansy general's with his nursery Eden, Pibble's with his ruined hero. And the rest of life wasted to non-existence. Ridiculous! Suppose Mike were to discover, now, that Pibble had been lying, a victim of half-senile fantasies, all he would feel would be disappointment, and perhaps pity. His life would not be in any way changed, so why should Pibble's be? That was all over, long ago. Over. Over.

Motionless under the light bedclothes Pibble sensed through all his being a surge of moral energy. It seemed to tingle along clogged arteries, as well as through his mind. He was going to give up Foyle. The sensation was brief, and faded.

Like giving up smoking, he thought. Yes, very like, in that it probably wouldn't really happen—certainly not without relapses—but still the decision had been made, and that was that. Henceforth he would know, even in mid-wallow, that Foyle was an excuse, a crutch which could be thrown away. No one had cheated Pibble. He had lived a life of richness and variety, and his many failures had turned out lucky ones. He was like that seventh son who, lolling along the unobstructed path to hell, still manages to fall over his own feet and so stumble into heaven.

Though the moral impulse had dwindled like a wave down a beach, its effect remained. It had wetted the sand, so that what before had been dry and random drift could now be shaped and built with. He decided to think about Jenny, objectively.

What would be best for her? Correct examination answer: a man of her own age, sensitive and lively, who could gentle out her knotted horrors and let her become . . . become what? More herself, or less? Different, anyway. And she was all right now, surely. The image of her was strong in his mind, the easy, humming happiness, a balance achieved against the odds, like that of a toy gyroscope, humming on its wire. Yes, all right now . . . but in ten years' time? Jenny at forty, brisk but twitchy, mistress perhaps of a hundred beds, on which lay a hundred poor old vegetables. And at home, what? What home? He could envisage only a clean and colourless space, half a life quite cauterised. By then the toy would be beginning to precess towards its eventual fall.

But suppose he, Pibble, were to perform for himself the necessary miracle—make the shadow go back ten paces down the steps of the temple—and become . . . oh, no, not that imaginary young man, but a person again, for a few years something other than an object of pity or disgust, could he then help her? Would she be worse, or better, for his company?

Supper came. Mrs Finsky snapped him into wakefulness, and he ate with pleasure. For a while after that he listened to the radio, but a talk on Australian business ethics brought on a bout of Foyle-brooding (it sounded as if Dickie would have been quite at home among those twang-vowelled venturers) and he drove it away by returning to Jenny. He had reached no conclusion when heels clicked on the parquet beyond the door. The door itself gave its rich whimper, and Maisie was floating across the room towards him.

"I've come to put you to sleep," she said, childishly solemn.

His mind seem to slip its clutch and not quite recover. Subconsciously he had been expecting Jenny, to renew and reaffirm his picture of her not as a poor neurotic girl but as someone who had a perfect right to be exactly what she was; so to be confronted by this other creature, who perhaps did not have that right but certainly needed help of a quite different sort . . .

"Jenny?" he croaked.

"Jenny's got a headache. She says she's got a headache."

Of course. Rather than bring on one of Maisie's "fits" by saying that Pibble wanted to interrogate her, Jenny had simply asked her to do the night round, and left the problem to him.

"I don't feel sleepy," he said. "You're early, aren't you? I want to talk to you."

"Not now. I'll give you your sleep medicine."

"Maisie . . ."

"I've got all the others to do."

"It won't take long. You've plenty of time."

But she'd already turned to the drug cupboard. For a moment he saw her reflection in the mirror that concealed it, as she stood and stared at herself as though she were a stranger. He remembered the ghost that had gazed at him out of the other mirror, the night of the murder, the seemingly quite other existence . . .

She clicked the catch of the mirror and swung it down, so that it became a shelf on which she could measure out the doses. The image of the doppelganger stuck in his mind, the creature that walked while she slept.

"How's Lord Hawkside getting on?" he said.

"He's dead."

"Dead!"

"Marianne killed him."

"I thought . . ."

She turned and he saw that the doppelganger had come out of the mirror and was now sleep-walking towards him, carrying the little tray with the medicines on it.

166

"Wake up, Maisie. You can wake up now."

No change. *You can wake her up if you yell at her.* No. that would bring someone in, and spoil his chance. She settled the tray on to the bedside table—three white pills, two mauve capsules and a green one; his glass of sleep-medicine, or what looked like it; everything normal.

"Tell me about your dream," he said.

"Not now."

"It's dark. There's a storm outside the castle windows. No furniture in the room—only one long chair and a stove. Lord Hawkside . . ."

He thought the hand holding the thermometer hesitated for an instant before she thrust it into his mouth and silenced him. He lay gazing up at her strange face, made stranger by foreshortening. Where had he seen it? Not in life, somehow. A book-cover? A poster? Yes, a drawing of some sort . . . Beardsley? Something like that; in the background the hunch-back domino and the grinning gross page-boy, and filling the foreground a few pure lines creating fold on fold of silk that swept up towards the tiny, sick-simple face and the monstrous aureole of hair. Something—a flicker of doubt or worry?—stirred beneath the trance-held features.

She finished taking his pulse and removed the thermometer. At once he started to speak in as leaden and unemphatic a tone as he could achieve.

"She's come through the storm to meet him. There is snow still on her cloak. He was watching her from the castle window. Her cloak blew round her like the wing of a bat . . ."

"Cold," she muttered.

"The wind is very cold. Chips of snow sting her cheeks. She reaches the door. It's dark inside. She shuts the wind out and climbs the stairs."

"Dust."

"Dust on the stairs, light shining in streaks through the slit windows. The first room's cold and empty. But the second room's warm, and he's there."

"Smiling."

"Yes, he's waiting for you, smiling. He's very handsome in the streaky light. He's wearing a frilly white shirt. Black breeches. Black boots. His gun is in its holster at his hip."

Her face rumpled into a frown. The smile vanished. He'd got something wrong. The gun?

"Not now," she said, aloud. "I've come to put you to sleep, Mr Pibble."

"Your dream, Maisie. Lord Hawkside and Marianne in the castle tower. He walks towards her, smiling, and undoes the clasp of her cloak. She's smiling too."

And she was, an actressy grimace, just as Jenny had said.

"Clothes," she muttered. "Kisses."

"He undresses her slowly, with kisses and caresses. She lets him do whatever he wants . . ."

"Do whatever he wants," she said, much more firmly, in a totally strange voice.

Pibble had begun to worry whether he was going to be able to keep the embarrassment out of his own voice as he traced her path through the erotic undergrowth, but now this other persona took over.

"As soon as you lie down you will go to sleep," it said. "As soon as you lie down you will go to sleep. You will sleep for exactly twenty minutes. You will be quite safe. No one will harm you."

There was a long pause.

"Marianne woke up," he prompted.

"Cold. Alone," she whispered.

"She was cold. There was no one else in the room. She got dressed. Where was the gun?"

"Pocket."

"The gun was in the pocket of her cloak. She held it. She left the room. Did she go up on to the roof?"

"Down."

"She went down the stairs and let herself out of the castle. She

168

left the door open, swinging in the wind."

"Maisie."

"She wasn't Marianne any more, she was Maisie. She let herself back into the staff wing and went up to her room. Jenny was there, drying her hair with Maisie's drier."

"Finished."

"Jenny saw the gun. Maisie told her about the duel in the castle. How did she know that?"

"Dream."

"Marianne had dreamed it while she slept? Somebody came while she was asleep in the castle?"

"Yes."

"But Maisie told me Marianne had killed Lord Hawkside."

Again her face rumpled. He felt the gossamer tackle with which he was trying to play her begin to break, so he let it go slack.

"Never mind," he said. "Jenny told her to say she'd been helping her wash her hair. She took the gun from her, and her cloak, and the key to the staff door. Was there only one key?"

"Only one."

"Who gave Maisie the key?"

"He did."

"Who?"

"Don't know! Don't know!"

Something was happening behind the mask of sleep. Suddenly the face contorted, as in a fever-dream. The small mouth opened to an O. Any instant the hoot would begin. Instinct reacted before caution could restrain him. He lurched himself up on to his left elbow and at the same time flailed his right arm, palm spread, towards her face. Before he made contact the darkness roared round him.

When he came too she was bending over him, smiling, normal, the doppelganger gone. He could see a patch of bright red on her left cheek.

"Jenny's got a headache," she said.

"Oh. Ur. Kind of you to come."

169

"You must have been asleep. I'll get your medicine, shall I?"

She turned towards the drug-locker. With fumbling speed he reached across to the bedside table and picked up the six pills, relaxing as he withdrew his hand beneath the bedclothes. She halted, gazing at the open shelf.

"Jenny can't have latched it properly," he said. "It fell open."

"Oh. Where's the tray?"

"Over here. She did me some sleeping draught, but I decided I didn't want it."

"All right. I'll bring your pills."

This time she took the three bottles off the shelf and brought them across to the tray, counting out the pills in front of him. He swallowed them one by one.

"Lord Hawkside's gone to France," she said. "That's terribly dangerous with a war on. He hasn't told anybody why."

"Wants to find something out, I expect. Wasn't that sister of his half-French?"

"Oh, yes. But you mustn't guess what's going to happen next. It spoils the surprise. Do you want to go to the loo while I make your bed?"

"All right. If you'll help me stand."

He felt strangely tottery, and realised that the day had been physically exhausting. Only the equally strange sharpness of perception deceived him into believing, until he tried it, that he should be able to strive and stride as he had ten years ago. Still, he managed to wrap the filched pills in a piece of lavatory paper without dropping any of them. He put the little packet into his pyjama pocket. Something was on his mind, a detail, buried now under the amazing leaf-fall of Maisie's dream-memories. He scuttered fretfully at it, found nothing. Only when he was lying back on his pillow, watching Maisie turn towards the door, did something—her movement perhaps—trip the right switch.

"Maisie?"

She stopped, half-turned.

"The metal detector," he said.

170

Now she turned fully and he saw she was the sleep-walker again.

"It's been through the metal detector," she said, dreamily, holding the non-existent parcel towards him.

"Did you put it through?"

"No."

"How do you know then?"

"Because it was in the tray?"

"Was it really in the tray?"

"It was in the tray. It's been through the metal detector."

"All right, I believe you. Good night."

"Good night."

As the door closed he realised that she had forgotten to dim the lighting. He lay for a little, summoning up the will to rise again, and when he achieved it took advantage of being up to empty his sleeping-draught down the basin, and to tuck the twist of pills into the drawer where his socks were kept. Lying again in the dimness he regretted the sleeping-draught. He was far from sure that there was anything wrong with the pills, and thought it even more unlikely that a liquid would have been substituted, but perhaps he should have kept it. Or drunk it.

Clearly, he wasn't going to sleep. His brain was too busy, had built up a momentum which would become a churning reiteration unless he channelled it into useful work. He tried to remember a long-ago text-book on hypnotism, borrowed from a library in order to settle an academic argument with poor Ned Rickard. Fragments still adhered, like wisps of fleece in a hedgerow. Soldiers can be hypnotised en masse with great ease because they are already drilled into obedience of the meaningless. A particular Private, subject of a demonstration before senior officers, is told under hypnosis that when he leaves the room he will turn the light off. He is put through various tricks, then woken and told he can go. Hesitates at the door. "You were wanting the lights off, sir?" "No." With an awkward bob of shame he flicks the switch off, despite his waking orders, and scurries away. Not very relevant?

171

What about the woman, subject at a demonstration before students? Lecturer called away, leaving her under hypnosis. Students find that they can carry on, persuade her she's a hen or a bishop, but when they try to get her to take her clothes off she has hysterics. Um. Cases only. Must be as much variability as there is in the human mind. Maisie was almost indefinitely suggestible, and by almost anybody . . . Jenny, after all, had managed to impress on her the notion that she had been helping with the hair-washing, and thus actually remove the imprint of the earlier belief that she herself had shot Tosca . . . a slippery tool, liable to twist in the hand . . . but one would be aware of this. Like a computer programmer one would try to build in security sequences, so that a stranger attempting to tap sensitive material would cause the whole mechanism to reject its orders . . . Pibble had tripped such a mechanism when he had asked too insistently about the key . . . yes.

But would she have killed? Would she have done a murder? All the books said no, pointing to the woman who had refused to undress for the students. On the other hand there was the Private who had disobeyed the direct order and turned the light off. How could the books be sure? There were enough experiments, Pibble remembered, to show that subjects refused to do things which their waking intelligence would have told them were harmful to themselves. They might be prepared to lock their bodies into a rigidity they could never have achieved under their own will-power, but they still wouldn't put their hands into boiling water.

What about moral repugnance? Take somebody who is a potential murderer in any case; presumably he could be hyp-notised into a killing. Or take the woman who had had hysterics when the students tried to get her to strip; if that woman had lived in a less tabu-ridden era, or had been a different woman—had been Maisie? Perhaps even Maisie wouldn't have done it for the students; but for Lord Hawkside? *The only people she's ever been properly in love with are the heroes in her toshy books.* But in that case, couldn't she have shot him? Suppose Tosca had been cast in

172

a different role—the villainous Sir Jasper Fence—wouldn't Marianne have killed him for her lover's sake? An idea like that seemed to have been planted at some time in the mess of her mind, and then not quite erased. Murder by proxy. Extraordinarily tempting if you had the power. Tempting to see whether you had it, to play with the curious toy . . .

Despite apparent wakefulness, he slept.

Eleven

THE QUALITY OF sleep had changed. He experienced a strange sense of return, not the honeyed dream-return to the gardens of childhood, but simply to the sort of sleep he had enjoyed for most of his life until his illness took him. Light, but not restless, aware of noises and movements, aware that dreams were only dreams. When he woke it was because somebody had come into the room, and before he opened his eyes he knew who it must be, and why.

"I'm not dead," he whispered.

"No?" said Toby Follick, interested as ever, as though the lack of deadness were an unusual and fascinating symptom. He opened the bathroom door and pulled the light string, shooting a beam of yellow across the bluish darkness. He checked that the door screened the inspection-panel, just as Pibble had checked on the night of the storm, then came with eager little steps to the bedside.

"You ought to be asleep," he said. "It's a quarter to two. You didn't take your medicine?"

"I didn't take the pills, either."

"Oh? What did you do with them?"

"Flushed them down the loo. Maisie got me some new ones and I took those."

"Good, good. You're very on the spot these days, James."

"I suppose I am . . ."

Follick nodded, as though this had been just what he expected, a trick that for once had gone according to instructions. He turned, picked up the folder of graphs that charted Pibble's dotage, carried it to the bathroom door and studied it, holding it aslant to catch the yellow light. Pibble watched him. Nobody could have looked less sinister—a neat, brisk little man, pleasing and self-pleased. His feet were in shadow, but it was inconceivable from the rest of his proportions that they were not neat and small also.

"Remarkable. Lovely," said Follick. "If we carry on like this we'll get you into the reference books."

He closed the folder and brandished it as though it were a peace-treaty brought back to a rejoicing people.

"Ur?" said Pibble, feeling that the performance had strayed into an unrehearsed routine.

"How are you feeling after the day's excitements, James?"

"Not too bad. Tired, quite tired . . ."

"Only to be expected."

"But not stupid."

"Splendid. Ready to face the world?"

"Yes. Yes, I think so."

Pibble could hear a note of surprised recognition in his own voice.

"We'll soon have you out of here," said Follick, with no hint of ambiguity in his tone. "Tell me, what's this about not taking your pills?"

"Maisie came round. She was in a sort of trance. I was afraid they might be, um, doctored."

"Why on earth should you think that?"

"A lot of reasons."

Follick nodded and came back towards the bed. Automatically, he made as if to flip the folder back on to the table, but stopped in mid-movement and replaced it with precise care in the place it had come from, then stood tapping it with his forefinger.

"I did it," he said suddenly.

"I know."

"You can't know, James. You were under hypnosis—only just

under, but enough."

"Uh? I thought you were talking about . . ."

"The improvement in your condition, James. It's early days, of course, but if we carry on as we've begun you'll be leading a pretty well normal life by mid-summer. The point is, you can't do it without my help."

"Ur?"

"That's right. I can give you a life worth living, for at least another five years—quite a bit more, with luck."

Now watch carefully, ladies and gentlemen. My assistant here what has had the misfortune to get hisself sawn in half, I will put the pieces of into this here chest—quite empty, no deception—and close it up—so!—and make a few magic passes what I learnt from the mystic sages of the East—the East, sir, not the East End—and open the chest up again—so!—and what do we have? One walking, talking, all-in-one-piece young feller-me-lad! Legs on the right way round, sonny? Good-oh! Well go and sit back down among the audience and we'll get on with bringing back that lady what vanished ten minutes ago. Thank you, thank you, ladies and gentlemen!

"I believe you have plans, James?"

"Uh?"

"Or if you don't, Jenny does."

"Oh! Did Maisie . . ."

"My spies are everywhere. Let's not go into that. Now, you're a good egg, James, not a wheedler or a whiner. I can't see you setting up house with Jenny or whoever if you think you're going to be a thorough nuisance to her. You're never going to be young, of course; you'll always have a bit of trouble with your legs, but you can control that with the right drugs . . . Put it this way—you won't want Jenny coming home from a long day among the stretcher-cases to find another one waiting for her? No, of course not. But that's what it'll be if you don't let me help you. How much do you know about hypnosis?"

"A bit."

"Then you may know that it works much better with the young

176

than with the old. That's why I don't make much use of it here at Flycatchers. I only stumbled on the fact that I could do it at all, by accident, a couple of years back. Naturally, I got pretty excited, and read it up, and talked to doctors who use hypnosis for therapy, and so on. I found out that I'm a natural—I mean that even knowing nothing about it I could put people under when more experienced chaps had failed with them—so I thought I'd try on one or two appropriate cases down here. But it wasn't much cop. Too old, too bloody obstinate. And I'm good—I really am, James. I don't think you're likely to find anyone else who can help you the way I can. You follow?"

"Yes."

"And the alternative's not very nice, is it? I've seen people like you fairly often—not honestly much wrong with them physically—just given up. They go to pieces in a way which doesn't seem to happen to the ones with honest-to-God physical illnesses—you've been there once, haven't you, James?"

"You came to tell me this in the middle of the night?"

"Explain about that in a minute. I've been thinking a lot about you, James, trying to work out what makes you tick, and how I can help you. I want to clear something up first. When you went out to the tower that night, it wasn't because you'd heard any shots, was it?"

"You know the answer."

"What? . . . Oh . . . Well, let's take it you didn't hear any shots. You'd decided to put an end to yourself, and you'd decided to do it that way, partly because it's not all that easy killing oneself in a place like Flycatchers, and partly because you wanted us all to realise that you knew what you were doing. As I said just now, you'd been down into the depths, and we'd hauled you back, and that was your way of making sure while you still had the will-power that you didn't go down there again. I must say, I think it was a pretty good performance. I hope I'll have the guts when my time comes. But as a matter of fact it was that which made me realise that I might be able to help you. You were ready to be

177

helped."

"You knew I hadn't heard a shot?"

"I worked it out."

"You knew."

"What do you mean?"

"You fired the gun. Earlier."

Follick shook his head, but rapped the folder a couple of times as if to reassure himself that it was there.

"Not me," he said. "Maisie."

"No," said Pibble.

He was full of a curious floating elation, an almost loony cheerfulness, as if he had taken a perception-enhancing drug. Everything was going to work out with lovely tidiness. Follick would kill him, thus solving his own dilemma. Jenny would find the pills among his socks, take them to Mike . . . Cass was already constructing his case from the other end, among the old death-certificates . . . he and Mike would meet in the middle like teams of tunnellers . . .

"I can't argue with you until you tell me what you're getting at," said Follick.

"All right. Tosca. Policeman. Wilson's bodyguard. I don't know if he'd gone wrong before he came here . . ."

"We may have pushed him over the edge. There's a lot of money about, and it sometimes has that effect. I don't think we'd have taken him on the staff if he hadn't been landed on us."

"It doesn't matter. He may have been snooping around for pickings, or he may have stumbled on it by accident . . . about six weeks ago he was trying to get off with Maisie. He'd made a list of all the nurses and he was seeing how many he could lay. He was that type. Maisie's a very good hypnotic subject—that's how you discovered your abilities—and Tosca triggered her somehow into a trance, in which she told him something about the death of a patient here, Sir Archibald Gunter . . ."

"Maisie did that. I was in the States."

"Yes. Maisie did it because you told her to, and you arranged to

178

be in the States because you were getting worried about the deaths at Flycatchers. It was becoming known that this was a good place for the disposal of the elderly rich, and you needed to set a scapegoat up. My guess is that the first deliberate death was that of a man called Foster-Banks. I think it was suggested to you by the other shareholders that he had to be disposed of, and you arranged it. The trouble was that there were then a few very influential people who saw no reason why they too shouldn't take advantage of this new service, provided by Flycatchers, so you began to feel trapped. When you discovered how obedient you could make Maisie . . ."

"You really don't understand about her!"

"She can't always have been like she is now. She'd never have passed her examinations, let alone got taken on the staff of a crack place like this. Don't you think that although she was always, uh, susceptible, you've changed her? There must have been some controlling mechanism, to get her through life this far. But I think you've broken that down. She's pretty well a schizophrenic now, isn't she?"

"Not me," said Follick, puzzled but unperturbed. "I've been trying to help."

Pibble drew a long, restful breath. He had been speaking in the quietest possible tones above a whisper. It was as though his physical being was a fine electric filament, capable of carrying only a particular current. Any surge of energy might burn it out. But the current was there, flowing steadily, in a way that it had not done for months, so that the filament could glow with a clean, unwavering light.

"I don't think so," he said. "When you discovered your hypnotic gift, I think you were probably teasing her about her romantic novels, pretending that she was one of their heroines— something like that—and you found you'd put her into a state in which she thought it was true. By now, you and Tosca between you have done it so often that her fantasies have become as real for her as her everyday existence. When Tosca started to put

179

pressure on her, she retreated into that world as a sort of defence mechanism—that's how he found out about it—and naturally he took it into his head to explore a bit further, and discovered what had happened to Sir Archibald. Being Tosca, he didn't hesitate to try and blackmail you. He got somebody—an old woman, apparently—to write a letter to the local police, so that they should come and see you and make you jumpy. Your first reaction was to make sure it didn't happen again. You planted in Maisie the order that if anyone started to ask her questions about certain things she was to refuse to answer, and come and tell you. It happened again this evening, which was why you told her to bring me the doctored drugs.

"But you still had the problem of Tosca. You had to get rid of him—kill him. It wasn't going to be as easy as doing away with one of your patients. Tosca was armed, strong, on guard. Then he played into your hands. He was genuinely concerned to seduce Maisie—that would be important to his own image of himself—and he took it into his head that he could force you to help him. He'd enjoy that, too. You explained that even in hypnosis Maisie wouldn't make love to him, because there are limits and inhibitions the hypnotist can't overcome. You hit on the idea that Tosca would have to become part of her dream world in order to make it work, and to do that the full romantic trappings would be necessary—the fancy dress, the tower, the storm. It probably *was* necessary, but it had other advantages; it would pin the murder on Maisie; the noise of the storm would drown any shots; it would be enough time before the body was found to cover any minor clues; and so on. As the doctor who does the liaison with the security side, you've got a set of keys, haven't you?"

"Er . . . as a matter of fact, yes. Maisie knows where they are."

"You would make sure of that. You've thought it out in detail. If Maisie was going to seem to have used the keys she would have to know where to find them, but in fact you gave her the key to the staff door, and you set about persuading her to go to the tower. I think you experienced a little difficulty here. You weren't at all

180

sure whether she would allow Tosca to go as far as you needed, so your first idea was to cast him in the role of the villain, who would be attempting to ravish the heroine when the hero turned up and challenged him to a duel and killed him. But she must have rejected that, so you re-cast the plot and Tosca became the hero, and she went out in the storm to meet her lover. She's still got both ideas mixed up in her mind, though.

"I expect you'd taken advantage of Tosca's watch-periods in the tower to search his room—you'd have the key for that, too. You wanted to check whether he'd left any message, just in case; but you'd noticed that he had unusually small feet for a man of his size, and shoes that you could wear. That seemed to make the whole thing possible. You could go to the tower too, and leave no footprints of your own.

"That day there were plenty of gale warnings on the wireless—I heard them, because I was . . . never mind. You made contact with Tosca and told him to expect Maisie that evening. You put Maisie into a trance and told her what to do . . ."

"It can't be done, James. You don't have to take my word for it. I could show you half a dozen books."

"I know, but you solved that problem by programming Maisie to fall asleep as soon as she lay down. That could be done, and it's, uh, *right*, if you see what I mean. From what she tells me, the sort of book she reads isn't exactly straight-laced, the way they used to be, but it still draws a veil over the actual bedroom scenes. There was another advantage—two, in fact. Part of the idea was to distract Tosca's attention, so that you could get at his gun, and I can't think of anything much more distracting than . . . uh . . . well . . . On top of that was the problem of Maisie's memory. I got her to talk a little about it; with part of her mind she does remember what happened, and you couldn't risk that."

"When schizophrenics want to deny responsibility for things they've done they usually persuade themselves they were asleep."

"Exactly. That would make it look as if Maisie had in fact shot Tosca, but it doesn't explain why she took him up to the roof to do

181

so."

"She got the gun and he ran away and she followed him."

"Up? And through a bolted door? And then two shots from close range in the back of the head? No, he was held up, and marched up there, so that the shot shouldn't wake Maisie. I think you'd rather have killed him in the room, so that she could wake up and find the body and the gun and think she'd killed him herself. Part of the whole idea was that it would dispose of Maisie too, not by killing her, but by having her put away and her 'dreams' regarded as part of her psychiatric problem, but you couldn't take the risk of her seeing you. As a matter of fact, the way Tosca was killed was much more characteristic of a gangland shooting."

"This is all nonsense, James. It's impossible to say that a schizophrenic will or will not behave in a certain way. Now I'm going to tell you what really happened . . ."

Pibble's lips mumbled his willingness to listen, but already the current was fading, fading, and his mind was full of shadows. Vaguely he followed the thread of Follick's talk . . . Maisie suddenly saying under hypnosis that she had killed Sir Archibald Gunter, she didn't know why . . . Follick believing that she was fantasising, that his treatment was helping her, only gradually discovering that with a schizophrenic's unconscious cunning she was deliberately dragging him into the web . . . then dragging Tosca in as well, so that the two of them could buzz and grapple while she watched . . . no knowledge of why she shot him . . . Tosca too violent for the fantasy, perhaps . . . but Follick's own career, and the cover-up over Gunter . . . Only when Wilson died . . . if she could be persuaded to tell Pibble, then perhaps Follick might not be caught in the final destruction of the web . . .

It was conjurer's patter, and had that manic energy about it, rising steadily to a climax which at last forced Pibble into full awareness.

". . . couldn't sleep," Follick was saying. "It was all rattling round inside my head until I got up and checked the drug-safe, just for something to do. She must have had another key, James. She'd used mine before, but had given it back quite willingly when she told me about Gunter. I should have guessed. She'd got it copied . . . Believe me, James, I came to check on you, yes, but not to see if you were dead—to see if you were alive!"

Follick's tones were full of energy and excitement, but they breathed no sympathetic life into Pibble. No, he thought, it won't wash. Maisie told me, tonight. She hasn't cut that side of her off. And the pills—she didn't know what she was doing—she took new ones from my cupboard; and the shoes, glowing like beetles but fitting into no conceivable romantic fantasy; and the shots in the back of the head; and Wilson, yes, Follick had actually asked how long the police would hang around, and Pibble had told him that if Wilson left . . . and more than all that there was the actual conversation, now in this room. Suffused through Follick's apparent worry and fear was that throb of excitement, almost of delight. It was the quickness and ingenuity of the argument that thrilled him, the sheer sleight-of-mind, whereby the object which the audience sees—the goldfish bowl or the bunch of paper flowers—seems to remain in full view all the time but between a blink and a blink it has become a white dove, fluttering round the room, free.

"I need your help, James," said Follick, tapping the folder as if for emphasis. "I need Jenny's too, and you've got to help me persuade her. Between you you've got to undo the damage you've done by providing Maisie with a false alibi. I'm not talking about damage to me, or even damage to Flycatchers, but damage to Maisie herself. You see, she's got to have treatment, and she's got to have it in a place where they can make sure she does no further harm. She won't be punished—she's eminently certifiable—but really the best thing that could happen to her now is for the authorities to know that she killed Tosca and caused Wilson's death. Then they'll take her seriously. She can be shut up and looked after and perhaps even cured. But that's as far as we need go. I can see no point in raising the question of Sir Archibald's death. Once Maisie is being looked after we can be confident that sort of thing won't happen again . . . But listen, James, this matters to you as much as it does to me. You see, if it comes out that I was covering up for Maisie, I shan't be able to practise any more, and that means I shan't be able to help you. Don't you see? With my help you can start to live a normal . . ."

Pibble had ceased to listen. Follick had dropped his voice to the tone of deadness, deadness somehow suffused with power, which he had adopted for hypnosis, but for Pibble only the past was present. All this had happened before.

"These are very serious allegations, Inspector."

"Yes, sir."

The large office, strange-seeming for the Yard, with no more than two or three loose files in one tray and some signed letters in another on the wide desk. Beyond the windows a clatter of trams on the Embankment, and then the Thames sliding greasily through the dusk-like noon of winter. The man at the window looking out at the view, as if turning his back on the problem Pibble had brought him. A weak man, rumour said, a stop-gap. Certainly the office had an hotel-like feeling of being unimpressed by its occupant, but of course that made him more formidable, in that he stood not for himself but for the Yard, in its complexity and secretiveness and vacillation. Pibble was aware that he himself was of the same kind, and that in the impossible event of promotion to this room, he himself would react with the same fret and indecision to such a heaving-up of stones.

The man turned from the window.

"I take it you have thought of your own position," he said.

"Yes, sir."

"If we do not institute this inquiry you suggest . . ."

"I should have to resign, sir."

"And then?"

"Try to do something from outside, sir."

"We can't afford . . . even though . . . no . . . This couldn't have come at a worse time . . ."

A longer pause.

"Let me put my cards on the table, Inspector. You have so far named no names, and quite right, but of course I am aware that the main target of your allegations is a very intelligent and popular officer. Popular with the public, too. To put it bluntly, we can't afford to lose him, and to put it even more bluntly, we can afford to lose you. You understand?"

"Yes, sir. I will send in my resignation tomorrow."

"It needn't come to that. There is a middle way—there usually is, you know. A number of senior posts are due for re-allotment, and though the officer you refer to was not on the list of names for consideration, there is no reason why he should not be included. He could, in effect, be promoted in such a way that if your allegations are well-founded he would do no further harm, and if they are not he would have received a reward he well deserved."

"But . . ."

"One moment, Inspector. I asked you just now about your own position. I know you to be an intelligent and hard-working officer, and those are valuable qualities. But there is another quality which here at the Yard we value even more, and that is loyalty. All of us, at one time or another, have to accept decisions that go against our interests, or our judgment, or our private conscience. In asking you to accept the course I suggest, I am asking you to demonstrate your loyalty. Because of your war service you have fallen a little behind some of your contemporaries in the promotion race but it is not too late to catch up, and even overtake them. You follow me?"

"Yes, sir."

"And what do you say?"

"No."

"No."

The syllable was like an echo, whispering back from the cliffs of the past. It hung in the sick-room, answer to a question that Pibble was not even aware of having heard. In the silence heels clicked twice on the parquet outside the door. Neither Pibble nor Follick stirred until with a slight scrape they moved away across

185

the soft carpeting. The fire-door sighed. The room relaxed, breathed.

"No, James?"

"I don't believe you."

"Why on earth not?"

"Too many reasons. I'm tired now. You killed them all; Tosca, Wilson, only trying to frighten him off, Foster-Banks, two or three others. Got an account somewhere—Switzerland. They'll find it."

"You *are* tired James. My fault—I shouldn't have kept you talking so long. You'd much better sleep on it, give the old brain a chance to recover. The blood's got to get to the brain, remember?"

"I remember," said Pibble, unamazed.

Follick gave the folder a final tap and came towards the bed.

"I've brought one of my eight-hour knock-outs," he said.

His hand made a pass in front of his breast pocket and a hypodermic syringe gleamed between his fingers. Pibble lay still and watched him perform the ritual of raising it to the dim light and squeezing out the first drop. He made no resistance as Follick peeled back the bedclothes and folded the pyjama sleeve up the scrawny arm. Now, now it would end. And Jenny was only a couple of rooms away, putting Lady Treadgold to sleep.

As if the image of her had been a primeval stimulus, jerking the body into unwilled action, his other arm threshed across the bed. Before he knew what he had done his hand was gripping Follick by the wrist, pushing the needle away. After the first judder of surprise, Follick reacted without apparent emotion, one hand holding the target arm to the bed and the other simply forcing the needle towards it against Pibble's resistance. He seemed immensely strong. Though Pibble's arm-muscles were the least wasted in his body, they were like paper, fluttering against concrete. When the needle was an inch above the flesh he jerked it across and as Follick resisted, back. The frail point plunged nearly to the sheets, but impassively Follick heaved it up and over the target again. Pibble's heart was thundering and bubbling. He could sense the darkness closing, closing. Any moment it would

186

roar round him, drown him, and the last thing he would know of life would be this senseless struggle. Too concentrated on the effort to cry out he raised his eyes to Follick's face, and as he did so Follick seemed to grow an extra arm, monstrous, from behind his shoulder. The arm closed round Follick's neck. For an instant Pibble saw the small round hand clench with effort, and then Follick's wrist was wrenched from his grasp. The face disappeared. The weight vanished from his arm. There was a heavy double thud and a gasp.

He rolled on to his side. Follick and Jenny were sprawling in a muddle of limbs across the floor, both threshing to rise. Follick managed it first, turned, stared for a moment at Jenny, and as she too was rising launched himself at her. His clenched fists beat down at her. She began to crumple.

Pibble rolled himself from his bed, and still gasping with the fall crawled across the soft carpet. As he reached the fight Follick drew back a foot to kick at Jenny who was now crouched on the carpet with her fore-arms covering her face. She was yelling. Pibble clutched at the swinging ankle, held, fell deliberately sideways. Unbalanced with effort Follick tumbled across him. His lips gasped "Run!" but there was no breath in his lungs to make the sound. Air croaked inward through his throat as Follick scrambled up. For a moment the creased, monkey-like face loomed over him, the mask, still untouched by anything more than a kind of eager surprise that life's whole performance should have gone so chaotically awry, but Jenny was still shouting incoherently, and as Follick turned to silence her, Pibble was aware in the motion of long-accumulated furies bursting into the open.

The motion was never completed. Over Follick's crouched back a metal structure gleamed, inexplicable, falling in a curve with the slowed intensity of action. He saw a cross-piece on the structure strike Follick, precise as a machine, on the nape of the neck. Still with the same treacle slowness Follick collapsed out of Pibble's vision.

Time resumed its proper beat. Lady Treadgold was standing above him in the gloom, an idol of triumph. She was wearing an orange bed-jacket, frothy with lace. Her head was almost bald. She panted, more with excitement than effort, as she lifted her walking-frame by its legs and held it high, ready to strike again.

"Stop shouting, nurse, and go and get help," she said. "There must be a policeman somewhere. Don't try to get up, doctor, or I'll hit you again . . . Oh, I wonder if I've broken his neck! Henry Cotton said I had a perfect swing, you know. I don't expect you had time to play much golf, Mr Pibble."

She pronounced the word *goff*.

Twelve

JENNY'S LEFT EYE was closed by a bruise which spread as far as her jaw-bone. She had a plaster across the bridge of her nose and another down her left cheek. She was moving very carefully still, as though not sure what was going to hurt. Pibble knew the feeling well.

"I ought to be nursing you," he said.

"I'm all right."

"Why did you come back?"

"I never went. I nearly came in straight away, but I didn't want you to think I was spying on you. I mean, you were probably in the bathroom, and that was all. I opened and shut the fire-door so that you wouldn't be worried and then I came back to listen. I could just hear your voices, then they stopped and there was a sort of grunting, so . . . ."

"He wouldn't have got away with it."

"No, but you'd have been dead."

"I suppose so. What brought Lady T?"

"Oh, she'd been waiting all evening to tell me about a grand slam she'd made, and when she heard the fire-door and I didn't come she got impatient and came to look for me."

"She's been in this morning. She showed me the dent on her frame."

"I hope it doesn't sound ungrateful, but I don't really like having my life saved. I expect you're used to it."

"It depends who does it."

"Exactly."

She had changed. The bruising and the plasters distracted only for a moment from a deeper alteration. He remembered his picture of her as the bud of a many-petalled flower, full of its own infolded energies. In a surreal slither of images the bud became a clenched fist, a child's round hand clutching its secret, and the secret was that she was afraid. She always had been, but now the tension that had held those small fingers so tight was slackening. She seemed to guess his thought.

"I never knew I could scream like that," she said musingly.

"No."

"I enjoyed it."

"Uh?"

"Well, not at the time, I suppose. I was scared stiff—for you as well as me. But afterwards, when I was lying in bed, waiting to go to sleep, I found I was feeling all jellyish and cosy and I realised what a lovely scream I'd had. I'm still a bit hoarse, you know."

"Going to do it more often?"

"No. No, I don't think so . . . Jimmy, why did Follicle . . . oh, I suppose I mustn't call him that any more. Bad taste. But why . . ."

"Don't know. When I was about ten, just after my father died, somebody gave me a pen-knife. There was a rope hand-rail up to the organ-loft in the chapel my mother joined. Greasy and fat. I started to cut it, and it seemed to flower. Lovely white fresh hemp opening up on both sides of the wound, like the seed-head of a dandelion. I couldn't stop. They took my knife away, of course."

"Just like a man. What's it got to do with Follicle?"

"I don't know—just guessing. Consequences of actions. Toby Follick, somehow . . . treated the world as if actions didn't have consequences. Everything you did was like a conjuring trick— when you've done it, that's all, and you go on to the next trick. But it isn't like that. Things have consequences. He kept having to invent new tricks to cope with the results of the one before."

"Rabbits all over the stage."

190

"Yes. Suppose for instance he killed Foster-Banks because he was destroying the set-up here, and suppose that he did it because one of the shareholders persuaded him to; after that somebody in that world would know that Flycatchers was a place in which you could dispose of old relatives in the kindliest possible way. So he'd be asked to do it again. And again. Those were the consequences. Perhaps he realised that he couldn't go on for ever; if more and more people knew it became more and more dangerous, so he invented a new trick. He found out that he could hypnotise Maisie, and he programmed her to kill Sir Archibald while he was on holiday. In the end she was going to carry the can for any future disposals, but then he ran into another consequence. Maisie told Tosca. And so on."

"Nothing ever ended."

"It doesn't."

The pause was like a rest on a walk through fog-bound fields, a vaguely-defined sphere of perception in which no possible ends presented themselves.

"Jimmy?"

"Ur?"

"Why did you go out to the tower?"

"Do myself in. Find an end."

"Why?"

"Knew I'd never have the nerve again. You'd given me the chance."

"I see. How did you think I'd react?"

"Unhappy for a bit. Get over it."

"I suppose so."

Her hand rose to caress the bruise on her jaw with stubby fingers, exploring the sensation with wary sensuality.

"What are we going to do?"

"Nothing. For the moment."

"I don't want to stay here. I'm going to start looking for another job."

"More old vegetables?"

191

"I don't know no, I don't think so."

"I've got to get myself well."

"Can you do that?"

"If I can't, no one can."

"You'll have to find somewhere to live."

"Yes."

"Mum still hasn't found a tenant."

"Uh?"

"It's quite nice. She wins prizes for her garden, you know. And the pub's only three minutes away. I think you could afford it. Shall I give her a ring?"

"Uh."

"OK, that means you've got three days to get yourself well enough for me to drive you over on my day off."

"Do my best."

Another of those pauses, only now the mist seemed to be clearing. Not that its vaguenesses were visibly tinged with sun, but still the walker might feel that if all went well the day could yet end serene.

"What are we going to say to Lady Treadgold? She's written for a Harrods catalogue. Last time she bought a wedding present it was absolutely hideous."

"What do you think?"

"That's not fair. You first."

She was looking down at her hands, spreading them wide open, stretched, as though she were trying to will her fingers into further growth.

"Things are a bit different, uh?" he suggested.

Her face didn't change, but he could feel the easing of tension.

"Nothing that happens here is real," she said slowly. "We'll have to start again if you're at Mum's, I'll see quite a bit of you I'll have to watch out for Mum, wooing you with clematis cuttings "

"We can't let Lady Treadgold be right about everything," he said.

THE END